THE CRUISERS

A Star Is Born

THE
CRU

WALTER DEAN MYERS

SERS

A Star Is Born

SCHOLASTIC PRESS • NEW YORK

To Ms. Leslie Cirko, a Special Education teacher who taught me about the problems of children with autism.

CHAPTER ONE

Sweets to the Sweet

"Zander, wake up!" Mom's voice drifting through the fog. "You've got a visitor!"

"Tell Kambui to come back later!" I said, my head still under the covers.

"It's LaShonda," Mom said. "She's really excited."

"About what?"

"About everything!" LaShonda's voice.

I peeked out from under the blanket and saw LaShonda Powell in the doorway. Her eyes were wide and her hair was standing in about four different directions. Before I could say anything she was sitting on my bed.

"Is this going to be okay?" Mom asked. "I don't need to chain anybody down, do I?"

"I just have to go over some things with Zander,"

LaShonda said. She had her knuckles rubbing the back of my head.

"I'll make breakfast for the two of you," Mom said cautiously. "You will be out to the kitchen soon, won't you?"

"Yes, ma'am," LaShonda answered.

Mom started out the door as I was trying to remember if I was wearing underwear. LaShonda had one arm around my shoulders and had her head close enough to kiss me if she wanted to. I was hoping she didn't want to.

"What's up?" I asked.

"I got a scholarship!" she squealed in my ear.

"Hey, that's mad good!" I said. "But you're in the eighth grade, what kind of scholarship are you getting?"

"Listen to this!" LaShonda cleared her throat and rattled the paper she held about three inches from my nose. "'Dear LaShonda Powell, We are pleased to offer you a full scholarship to the Virginia Woolf Society Program for Young Ladies based on your amazing designs for the play put on by the Cruisers last Wednesday. Completion of this program will qualify you for further scholarship aid to either Amherst, Spellman, or the Fashion Institute of Technology.' Zander, I'm going to college!"

"Right away?"

"No, but eventually," she said. She was sitting on the bed but still leaning on me. I knew that for LaShonda it was a special moment. For me it wasn't. I had to pee.

"People keep saying we're smart and everything," LaShonda said, her face against my shoulder. "But it takes more than being smart to go to college. It takes money for tuition and stuff like that, but it takes money for clothes, too. I need someplace where I can go to college and still work part-time to support Chris. If they pay my way to Fashion Institute, I'll have it m-a-d-e! I can get a part-time job and we'll both be right here in the city."

"That's good," I said. "But I got to go to the bathroom."

"Go ahead."

"I don't think I have any underclothes on," I said, knowing I didn't have any underclothes on.

"You sleep naked?"

"Yo, LaShonda, I have to pee. How about you getting out of the room so I can get dressed?"

She kissed me on the forehead and left the room, calling out to Mom about going to college.

LaShonda is real special. She's the kind of girl that will get your back if you have a fight, or design some clothes for you if you need them. She lives in a group home — I think it's Catholic — with her little brother, Chris.

I found my underwear on the floor, put it on, and then some jeans. I heard Mom and LaShonda talking as I went into the bathroom.

What was really going down with LaShonda was that her brother was quiet. Not just a little quiet but, like, he hardly ever said anything. I didn't know if he was slow or maybe had an emotional problem. Maybe it wasn't right, but even though me and LaShonda were homies, we never talked about her brother. I would have talked about him if she brought it up, but she didn't.

When I got out of the bathroom I went into the kitchen. Mom was making eggs and LaShonda was sitting at the head of the table just looking so pleased with herself it was good to see.

"Do you think you're a little young to be committing to fashion?" Mom asked. "You might change your mind and want to be a doctor or something."

"I want to be a designer," LaShonda said. "I've always wanted to do that, so this works out perfectly for me. I'll be a designer, make about twenty buckets of money, and then marry some cute boy."

"Like Zander?" Mom asked.

"No, I mean a *really* cute boy, with perfect teeth and a big car," LaShonda said. "And he's just going to adore me from head to toe."

"Zander, you want your eggs scrambled?" Mom asked.

I nodded and poured myself a glass of orange juice.

"Is Chris excited about it, too?" I asked.

"He doesn't get too excited about outside things," LaShonda said, her mood changing for an instant. "And I don't think he knows we're going to have to move, but he can deal with it."

"Where you moving?"

"They have the Virginia Woolf House on 141st Street. You remember where Dr. John Henrik Clarke used to live? We went there once during Black History Month?"

"Yeah, sort of," I answered. "Who's Virginia Woolf? She's, like, a civil rights lady or something?"

"No, she's a white British lady," LaShonda said, pushing some scrambled egg off her chin into her mouth. "She wrote a book called *A Room of One's Own*. It's about how women need to have their own space and whatnot. I read it. It was okay."

"So this is a black group that is interested in women's issues?" Mom asked.

"Uh-uh. This is a white group that is just starting a branch of their organization in Harlem," LaShonda said. "These eggs are good. I like real eggs. At our place we always get powdered eggs."

"They probably come from powdered chickens," I said.

"Zander Scott, why are you so stupid?" LaShonda asked.

"It's a man thing," Mom jumped in. "They try to keep it secret but it doesn't work, and every once in a while the stupid just pops up."

"Mom! You're supposed to be on my side," I said. "We are related, remember?"

"So you sent them your designs, and then what happened?" Mom asked.

"No, they came and saw the play that Zander wrote," LaShonda said. "I did the designs for the play because we didn't have the money to buy costumes."

"The thing you were writing on *Romeo and Juliet*?" Mom looked at me.

"Yeah, LaShonda made shirts and blouses for us," I said. "They were nice."

"I took oversize blouses and used material to add balloon sleeves and collars so that they looked a little Elizabethan," LaShonda said. "The girls had smaller sleeves and collars, but I tie-dyed the bodies and left the sleeves white. For the guys I made collars that were big and I put cardboard in them for shape. And their sleeves were solid white and pleated. They looked good."

"That's very innovative," Mom said. "Did you take pictures?"

"Kambui did," I said. "But it takes him forever to send stuff around."

"Mrs. Maxwell wants us to put the play on again sometime during the year," LaShonda said. She had finished her eggs and now ran her finger over the plate to get the last little bit. "I think the Virginia Woolf Society liked the play, too. Anyway, they said my costumes deserved recognition and they're going to give me a scholarship!"

I felt really glad for LaShonda because she is always for real. There isn't anything phony about her.

"You should publish the play — what's it called?" Mom plopped down and poured herself some coffee.

"*Act Six*," I said.

"You should change the name of the play and publish it in your paper," she said.

"There's a reason I called it *Act Six*," I said. "The original *Romeo and Juliet* has five acts. This is a one-act play that's a takeoff on the original."

"Nobody is going to know what it means, Zander," Mom said.

"I'll know," I said.

"And I'll know," LaShonda said, patting me on the hand.

Then LaShonda started talking about how she was going to start acting more mature. She had seen pictures of Virginia Woolf and said she looked like a real lady.

"Kind of proper looking," LaShonda added.

"Like us," Mom said, putting on her "proper" face.

"Yeah," LaShonda answered. "Like us."

THE CRUISER

A BAD IDEA COMES SAILING IN

By Kambui Owens

We are now reading two English newspapers online every day. They are *The Times* and *The Guardian*.

One big story in Jolly Olde England is that the English are thinking about letting kids who are 14 decide if they want to stay on an academic track or take up a trade such as retailing or repairing cars.

The Cruiser thinks this is a good idea, because kids who don't do well grade-wise will at least get something useful out of school. We could teach kids how to serve hamburgers at fast-food joints. Maybe get a degree in McBurgers and a minor in Chinese food.

This is one way of handling poor grades — teaching kids how to navigate dead-end jobs. I know some dudes who would be better off getting a PhD in sweeping floors rather than just sitting in the back of the classroom dreaming all day. This might even work for smart kids. I'd love to take up training to be Beyoncé's secret boyfriend.

Meanwhile, our own LaShonda Powell has been offered a scholarship by the Virginia Woolf Society. They must have seen her 360-degree dunk!

THE PALETTE

Get Serious, Dudes!

By Ashley Schmidt

When will the writers at *The Cruiser* finally take a subject seriously? Letting kids choose to opt out of academic studies at 14 is a serious question that will soon be considered over here. Kambui Owens might think he's being witty with his little remarks, but he's not, he's just irresponsible!

The Cruisers seem to think that just because they're individually smart they don't have to be responsible citizens of Da Vinci. Wise up, guys. Some subjects need completely serious responses! And if your so-called alternate newspaper doesn't stand for anything serious, why are you killing trees to publish it? Lastly, LaShonda's scholarship offer (and I actually interviewed her!) was for her design work, *not* basketball!

CHAPTER TWO

A Star Is Born

Sometimes things happen in this school that make me so proud of you all that every step I take becomes lighter." Mrs. Maxwell, our principal, had her hands clasped in front of her as she addressed the assembly. "And if any of you read the *New York Times* over the weekend you will know what I am talking about. In their new column, About Town, a *Times* reviewer mentioned the play put on by the Cruisers and was particularly delighted by the costumes designed by our own LaShonda Powell."

I don't know who started applauding for LaShonda, but soon the whole auditorium was on their feet. The review was already on Facebook, and parts of it had been tweeted a quadrillion times.

"And more good news is that the Virginia Woolf Society has stepped forward to offer LaShonda a scholarship to their academy. LaShonda, on behalf of the faculty of Da Vinci Academy, and from the bottom of my heart, I congratulate you on your designs and your wonderful talent. Please stand up and accept the school's appreciation."

LaShonda stood up and we gave her another round of applause.

"Yo, Zander, I think LaShonda's smile just got two inches wider," said Kambui, who was sitting next to me.

"It should be," I said. "Did you see what the *New York Times* said about her costumes?"

The next thing on the assembly agenda was a bunch of boring announcements about stuff that everybody already knew. All I was thinking was that the assembly had been called at the last minute and the first class of the day had been canceled. I hated to have Algebra canceled when I had actually done the homework.

"Zander, the C man wants to see the Cruisers in his office." Bobbi McCall pointed down the hall as we came out of the auditorium.

"What did we do now?" Kambui asked.

"He probably saw that all four of us were breathing at the same time," Bobbi said. "That's enough to send our assistant principal into orbit."

Me, Kambui, and Bobbi got to Mr. C.'s office first, and LaShonda, the fourth member of our merry band, came in a moment later. Miss Delgado, the new clerk, gave us a big smile and then motioned for us to go into the dreaded lion's den.

"Well, where do I begin?" Adrian Culpepper leaned back in his chair and adjusted his horn-rimmed glasses with the tips of his index fingers. "When you young people first came to my attention I thought you were a lost cause. But after several misadventures — so to speak — I see that there is a certain merit to your rather unorthodox methodology. I have called you here today not to admonish you but to encourage you to keep up the good work.

"I have not reached that stage of our relationship wherein I actually *like* any of you, but, as a group, you are not as reprehensible in my eyes as you once were. I thought you would want to know that."

"Oh, thank you, kind sir," Bobbi said.

"I must add that your attempt at journalism — if your pathetic little paper can be attached to that hallowed term — is still not my cup of tea, but it does show that you can spell most words. The important thing is that you occasionally bring a certain credit to Da Vinci Academy.

The piece in the paper reviewing Zander's play and, of course, your lovely costumes, LaShonda, is the kind of positive press I always hope for."

"Thank you, Mr. C." This from LaShonda.

Mr. Culpepper stood and shook hands with each of us and smiled.

"That's the kind of smile that a crocodile gets on his face just before he eats you," Bobbi said when we had left Mr. Culpepper's office.

"Crocodiles don't have faces," Kambui said.

"Who told you that?" I asked.

"People have faces," Kambui said. "Crocodiles do not have faces, and they don't have personalities, so they can't smile, either."

"Kambui's been reading *National Geographic* again," LaShonda said. "Once a year he comes up with something strange and you know he's been to the dentist and read *National Geographic*."

Kambui started going on about how he lived in the world of ideas and intellect, and nobody wanted to hear that so we started on down the hallway.

"You people just don't appreciate an intellectual," Kambui protested. "LaShonda appreciates me."

"No, I don't," LaShonda said.

"So who is this Virginia Woolf?" Kambui asked.

"She was all, like, 'Hey, women can think and write and get it on if we have a chance,'" Bobbi said. "She was on the front lines for women when people didn't know there was a battle going on."

"So what's that mean for LaShonda?"

"Two women came to our group home Sunday," LaShonda said. "They were talking about how they would let me come to their academy and learn to dress cool and act cool. Things like that. And then maybe later they would help me get into a school."

"They talking about serious money?" Kambui asked.

"Yeah," LaShonda said. "The way they ran it, all I had to do was to get busy with the grades and they could make it all happen. I got all excited and everything because I really hadn't put college on my map."

"You're going to Da Vinci, a school for the gifted and talented, and you didn't have college on your map?" I asked. "I can't buy that."

"Yo, Zander, I had it on my map, but I wasn't thinking it was a done deal or anything like that. You know, some people come in here with their father being a weatherman on television and their mother being a big-time model and they just know they're going to college. I was hoping, but I didn't have any guarantees. They're talking like they're going to make it happen."

"Zander is one of these people who don't worry about money the way the little people do," Bobbi said. "He just deals with the Big Issues, like world peace, global warming, and international terrorism."

"Bobbi McCall, shut up!" I said. "The only reason I don't worry about money for college is that I'm better looking, smarter, and have more talent than you people."

"Zander, if I shut up, where would you have to go to find wisdom in this small universe?" Bobbi said. "I am the heart and soul of the Cruisers, and you know it. That's why you always want to hang around me."

"Don't say that, Bobbi." LaShonda pulled an apple out of her backpack and started polishing it on her sleeve. "You don't want Caren to think you and Zander have something going on. She'll scratch your eyes out."

I wanted to tell LaShonda that her remark about Caren Culpepper was sick, but she had already made a sharp left turn and was headed down the hallway toward her second-period class.

The truth was that I was as proud of LaShonda as everybody else. And I was proud that old stuffy butt Mr. Culpepper had to acknowledge that the Cruisers had their stuff together. When he first called us into his office he was ready to kick us out of Da Vinci Academy, saying we weren't the kind of students fit for a gifted and talented school. He got on our case for not being in any extracurricular activities, and we made up our own club, calling ourselves the Cruisers. That was supercool, but our newspaper, which Mr. Culpepper liked to refer to as our "adventure into the writing trade," had found its place in our school. All the kids picked it up as soon as we published it, and Ashley Schmidt, the editor of the official school newspaper, *The Palette*, even said that it made that paper better.

Bobbi McCall was sharp. She was good at math and chess and was up on anything that dealt with women. Da Vinci Academy was in Harlem, but a lot of the kids at the school were white, including Bobbi.

Kambui Owens was my main man and into photography. Kambui was the kind of guy who had your back if things got wrong, but he would also let you know if he thought you weren't taking care of business.

LaShonda Powell did design, sewing, art, fashion, and anything connected with clothing. If you could wear it, she could hook it up. So when Mrs. Maxwell asked the Cruisers to do a short sketch of some kind for assembly, I wrote a one-act play based on *Romeo and Juliet*, and LaShonda designed the costumes. The costumes were smoking, too. She had everybody wear dark pants and then did individual tops for all of us. I liked mine because I looked good in it. The wide sleeves made me look like I was in an old movie or something, and I liked that.

Okay, I'm Alexander Scott. I think Mr. Culpepper likes me the least of any kid at Da Vinci because I'm the one kid he can't stare down. For one thing, I'm six feet and he's only five ten, and also because I'm good at staring people down. It's just something I can do. It's, like, a gift or something. What Mr. C. wants are kids who are grateful for walking in the door of Da Vinci and working hard every day to get a handful of A's. That's not me, and that's not Kambui, and not Bobbi, and not LaShonda. We cruise along, but we're smart and we know it.

Still, I was happy with the piece in the paper because LaShonda was right. College is a piece of cake if you have the money. My dad is a weatherman and pulls down good money, even if he is doing it out on the West Coast with his new wife. My mom is a model and sometimes an actress and we do okay. I would like to get a free ride to college just so I don't have to ask my father for anything. That's a different trip from where LaShonda is coming from and I know it, so I didn't say anything when she mentioned it. I know LaShonda's cool. She's all heart and fights better than Kambui.

On the way home I wondered what Mr. C. was thinking when he called us down to his office. Deep down inside of his stuffy butt I bet he was disappointed that he had to tip his hat to us.

THE CRUISER

I DON'T WANT TO BE NO LADY

By Bobbi McCall

Okay, like everybody else at Da Vinci I am glad for my homegirl LaShonda Powell. But I can't get with this "lady" business. Every time somebody puts a label on you they are restricting you in some way. A "lady" is supposed to do *this* or *that*, but in reality they are talking about what you are *not* supposed to be doing. If Rosa Parks had been a "lady," she wouldn't have gotten herself arrested. If Harriet Tubman had been a "lady," she wouldn't have been doing the illegal act of leading her people to freedom.

Virginia Woolf said that for a woman to write, she had to have her own money and her own space. In other words, she had to move away from what she was supposed to be doing as a "lady" and toward what her heart told her she needed to be doing.

And since I'm riding my high horse (Godiva-style if I so choose!), I will add one more thing. Only certain people in our society have been historically considered "ladies." Others were not allowed to reach that status. If the term "lady" can be given to you, it can also be taken away. Think about it!

And as for Ashley Schmidt and *The Palette* — I think she should work a little harder to keep that stuffy newspaper locked up so it doesn't leak any more hot air. *The Cruiser* will take care of itself.

CHAPTER THREE

All That Glitters . . .

I was happy because Culpepper finally had to admit that the Cruisers were the real deal, but when I got home Mom was even happier.

"Guess what happened today?" She looked at me all bubbly, like she was going to bring out a cupcake or something from behind her back.

"Yo, I don't know what happened today, and I don't think you should be throwing your television commercial smile at me," I said.

"I am not throwing my television commercial smile at you," she said. Then, with one motion, she flopped down into a cross-legged sitting position on the floor. "This is my television commercial smile."

Mom's a model and knows how to act and look pretty. When she threw her television smile at me it was good.

The woman was real good, and I could see why she was getting over on the tube. She had been working commercials for the past six months and raking in some heavy paper for a change. We spent it all real fast, but at least we had something to spend.

"So what happened today?" I asked.

"Two things." Mom held up two fingers like I wouldn't have understood the words. "The first was that I tried out for the part of the Gecko's girlfriend."

"The Gecko?"

"You know, the Gecko that sells insurance?"

"Yeah, but you're going to be his girlfriend?" I asked.

"It depends," she said. "They're going to run it by some good-doing black organization to see if they object to the Gecko having a black girlfriend. If they don't, I'll be his girlfriend and make a gazillion dollars."

I couldn't exactly wrap my mind around my mother being the Gecko's girlfriend, but the gazillion dollars sounded cool. I asked her what else had happened.

"Your father called me with an idea," she said. Now she had on her wait-until-you-hear-how-stupid-this-is expression. "He wants you and him to have face-to-face meetings once a week so he can mentor you. He's going to send us some equipment and you can see him on the Internet every Wednesday evening."

"I can see him on the net just by tuning in to the weather in Portland," I said. "Why do I want to see him on Wednesday evenings?"

"He said he wants to have eye contact with you so the two of you can talk about man kind of things," Mom said.

"What does he mean by man kind of things?"

"I don't know." She shrugged. "Maybe his new wife has taught him something."

That was cold. My parents have been divorced nearly five years and they're still sniping at each other. My dad, who is the super-duper black weatherman out in Portland, Oregon, is always trying to do *the right thing*. Sometimes I think he's got a book called *Corny Things That Fathers Need to Impose on Their Kids After the Divorce*. He's really all right, I guess, but if they're going to have a battle I'm always going to be on Mom's side. In any fight I always pick a side. That's just the way I am.

The Algebra homework sucked big-time. Mr. Manley (I should introduce him to my father), who was a substitute last year, is now teaching Algebra and he wants to make it a Black History class. Probably because he's black.

The first thing he did was to waste an entire period with the big news that the word "algebra" is from some Arabic word, and we were supposed to get excited about that. Phat Tony, one of the Genius Gangstas crew, asked if the dude who invented algebra was from Africa, and Mr. Manley said he was either from Africa or the Middle East.

"Probably a terrorist," Phat Tony said.

Everybody was agreeing to that, and Mr. Manley got really mad, which made the day a huge success.

Okay, I did the homework, checked my e-mails, ran through Facebook, checked out some blogs from Frederick Douglass Academy, answered some comments from Lower Canada Community College about American education, ate some meatball sandwiches (my mom's best supper next to mac and cheese), and was just about to hit the sack when Mom knocked on the bedroom door.

Usually when my mom wants to come into my room, she just throws the door open and bursts in, apologizing about how sorry she is to disturb me, et cetera, et cetera. She's never really sorry. She just doesn't care about my privacy, which she describes as an "issue" between us.

"The police are on the phone," she said. "Your friend LaShonda has a problem."

It was after eleven at night when we got a gypsy cab on the boulevard and took it downtown to the Port Authority building on Eighth Avenue and 41st Street. Mom stretched her legs out and told me what the police had told her.

"They found LaShonda and her brother on a bench at the Port Authority and the kids wouldn't give their names or address," she said. "When the police told them that they would have to take them to a shelter, LaShonda gave them your name and number."

"They have no idea why they were there?"

"No," Mom said.

"Did they say that LaShonda was . . . you know . . . all right?"

"I think she is," Mom said. "The police didn't sound angry or anything, just concerned."

We got to the Port Authority and it was crowded with people just milling around. Some looked as if they might have been waiting for buses, some looked homeless. The police are on the second floor, all the way back toward Ninth Avenue and in a corner. We went there and a round lady sergeant met us at the door.

"This is not the place for young kids to be by themselves," she said. "You know them?"

Mom said we did and we went into a room where LaShonda was sitting on a bench. Her arms were around her brother and he had his face turned away from us.

"You okay, baby?" Mom asked LaShonda.

LaShonda's head shook yes, but her eyes were saying no. Mom sat down on one side of her and I sat on the other, next to her brother. When Mom put her arms around her shoulders, LaShonda began to cry. I didn't know what to do except feel bad. I tried to take her hand, but her brother pushed me away.

Mom cradled LaShonda for a while, not saying anything, just patting the back of her head as my friend leaned against her shoulder. Sometimes — maybe most of the time — I didn't think much of just having a mother, but I was appreciating her as we sat there in the police station.

LaShonda and Mom talked quietly. I heard LaShonda saying how foolish she had been to think things were going to change so easily for them. Mom wasn't saying a lot, but she was comforting LaShonda. Most of all, I was looking at Chris.

Chris was, like, really good-looking. He had soft brown eyes and a nice mouth that made him look younger than I knew he was. He looked around the precinct room at the cops who passed by or at the clock on the wall. Occasionally, he glanced at Mom, but only from the side, as if he didn't want her to see him looking at her. What got to me most was his hands. They were always busy, moving from his chest to the tops of his thighs, and then to his knees before returning to his chest. The moves were merely touches, as if he had a thing — a ritual — he had to go through. And LaShonda, talking quietly to Mom, also moved with her brother, keeping his hands in the tight pattern he had set up, and away from Mom.

Once, a bell went off, and I watched Chris quickly put his hands over his ears. To me the bell hadn't been that loud, but I could see that Chris was in a different world than I was.

"You okay?" I asked him.

He looked away from me, down toward the floor.

"He's okay," LaShonda said, interrupting the sentence she had started to Mom.

LaShonda and Chris together, he going through a secret dance that only he knew about, she silently dancing with him, keeping him within the small space that only they understood, was something I had never seen before. It pulled at my gut, and I felt helpless and a little stupid.

LaShonda and Chris had been living in group homes for children — first Little Flower and then St. Francis, where they were now, and I wondered how long they had been going through this bit of her trying to keep him calm, and how much it was taking out of her.

"You need us to arrange transportation to a shelter?" the round sergeant asked. "The best we can do tonight is a shelter or have them sleep in the back of some precinct until morning."

"LaShonda goes to school with my son," Mom said. "Can we take them to our house?"

The sergeant knelt down in front of LaShonda and smoothed back my friend's hair.

"Baby, you haven't done anything wrong, but I don't want you to go anywhere you don't feel safe," the sergeant said. "Are you all right with going home with these people?"

"Yes, ma'am."

"How do you know them?" the sergeant asked.

"Zander and I go to school together," LaShonda said. "He's good people."

Yo, that got me all teary eyed.

The sergeant got my name and Mom's name and address and then said that LaShonda could go home with us. She asked how we were going and Mom said we'd take the train, but the sergeant went into another room and came back with enough money to take a taxi back uptown.

"What they said was that if I went into the Virginia Woolf program, then me and Chris would have to be separated," LaShonda whispered. "I can't let that happen. I just can't let that happen."

She said that her brother was autistic. I didn't know what that meant other than he was different. I was hip to not dumping on people who were different or who had things like autism or stuff like that, but I didn't really know what it was about.

But I saw the way LaShonda's brother clung to her. It looked like he was trying to get into her, to bury his head in her chest.

And she just held him. Like a mother holds a child. That's what I thought of when I looked at them in the darkness of the cab going through the streets, a mother holding a child.

Mom called the group home, and they were relieved. They said they would send somebody over to pick up LaShonda and Chris, but Mom said no, that they would stay with us overnight. She said that like she meant it, too. When the chips were down, Mom could man up with the best of them.

THE CRUISER

A GUEST EDITORIAL

By Phat Tony Williams

Yo, yo! Listen up. Today I had a visit to juvie jail to see what it is all about and to write an essay on what I saw. Well, what I saw was seriously foul. Me, Mr. Siegfried, and Caren Culpepper busted up to the Bronx to check out the facility. When we got in we saw a bunch of brothers lined up and we asked what they were doing. A guard said they were lining up to get their medications. He said, like, sixty percent of the inmates take drugs every day because of their problems. He even spelled it out — psychotropic drugs. I didn't run it too tough, but Caren asked if they were learning to use drugs, why shouldn't they use them on the street. The guard said that was just the way things are when you get put away.

This guest editorial has two things to say. Number one, I didn't know they had jails just for kids. I should have known that, but my mind really doesn't go there most of the time. Or any of the time. The other thing I have to say is that it looks like they're telling kids that sometimes drugs are okay.

So I was glad when we left, and I didn't want to write anything about what I saw or what I heard except that it made me feel sorry inside.

Lastly, there's some scary stuff happening out there in the world. Bad thing is that I don't know how to wrap my mind around it yet. Yeah, and peace to the Cruisers' paper that gave me the chance to say my say.

CHAPTER FOUR
My Brother's Keeper

I know a lot of people don't believe in God or Santa Claus or the Easter bunny. I don't think a lot about Santa Claus or the Easter bunny but I was hoping that God was real. The thing I thought was that there should be somebody enforcing the rules, and that the rules should be fair. When I see kids getting sick I think somebody messed up. When I see kids in jail, like in Phat Tony's essay in *The Cruiser*, I think somebody messed up really bad.

LaShonda and Chris needed to be together, and the way things were working out it didn't look easy. I thought about them being down at the bus station and then at my house and I felt sorry for them. It wasn't fair, and God should be about fair. That was all I thought that I wanted from life, just for it to be fair.

They slept on the couch in the living room, LaShonda with her arm around her brother, him not moving as he slept. I looked at them when I went to the bathroom and thought about a picture I had seen of two little children crossing a bridge at night with Jesus watching over them.

A lot of things must have been racing through LaShonda's mind. They were racing through mine, too, and I couldn't think of anything that looked like "something good to do." Everything looked hard, and maybe there weren't any really good answers. I thought that if God was real He should have come up with some good answers.

"So how come they have to separate LaShonda and her brother?" Bobbi asked. We were in the computer lab. She had her notebook on her lap and was doing chess problems. "If they've been together this long, why not just keep them together?"

"She said it's really a money deal," I answered. "It's cheaper to keep the boys in one place and the girls in another. So when this thing came up, with them offering LaShonda a special place —"

"Everybody jumped on it!" Bobbi looked up at me.

"Yeah."

"And now another sponsor has contacted the school, which complicates things even more," Bobbi went on. "Fragrance Perfumes is offering to contribute to the school's scholarship fund, and they want LaShonda to be the first one to get money from them."

"Yeah, that's what I heard."

"And Mr. C. wants us to meet with them in his office this afternoon to dance up and down and brag on the school, and your best idea is just to not show up?"

"Something like that," I answered, looking at her computer screen. "Try taking the knight."

"If I take the knight I can win a piece," Bobbi answered. "But the puzzle is a mate in two. Okay, I won't show up, but you know Culpepper is going to turn three shades of red and we'll all be in his office tomorrow."

I knew that, but I also knew we had to show LaShonda some love and some support. Mom had called St. Francis, where LaShonda and Chris were staying, and talked to the director there.

"They talked about some kind of spectrum," Mom said, rubbing cream on her forehead. "It depends on where a person is on the spectrum how well they're expected to do."

"How well is Chris expected to do?" I asked.

"They said they don't know," Mom answered. "Which isn't good, is it?"

"And what happens if he doesn't do well?"

"He might have to go to another kind of facility," Mom said softly.

At school I met Bobbi in the media center and told her what had happened at the Port Authority and what Mom had found out.

"She's got to take care of him, I guess," I added.

"So LaShonda can just say she doesn't want any part of the Virginia Woolf program," Bobbi said. "They can't make her do it, can they?"

"No, but she's thinking that maybe she won't be able to go to college at all," I said. "That's, like, a real possibility. People don't like to run it down like that, but there's no guarantee that everybody at Da Vinci is going to get over."

"Everybody here *should* get over," Bobbi said, making a move. "If they don't just because they don't have enough money, it sucks big-time."

Maybe nobody wanted to say it, but that's what it looked like. Mr. Marcus, our science teacher, said that he always questioned longevity rates, which said that poor people just happened to die earlier than people from richer groups.

I didn't know what to do, really. Bobbi was definitely on time thinking kids shouldn't get messed around just because they didn't have a lot of money, but I knew how things rolled in the real world.

I didn't know how to feel, either. Except maybe sad.

At home, Mom made a stir-fry with hamburger and frozen veggies and it came out terrible. Some of the veggies were still cold and the hamburger tasted nasty. She said it wasn't that bad and then when I didn't eat it she got on her hurt look.

I put my plate in the microwave and zapped it for two minutes. It didn't taste any better, but at least it wasn't cold.

Somehow they let Kelly Bena, the smartest girl in the school, read the announcements. Actually, they can make anybody in the school read them, but usually they won't let Kelly because she deliberately messes them up.

"The girls' soccer team will meet in the boys' locker room at three-oh-five," she announced. "Make sure you bring your equipment, which will include —"

The mike went dead for a minute and I knew somebody in the office had shut it off. Then Kelly came back on.

"Okay, it's the *boys'* soccer team that will meet in their locker room at three-oh-five," she said. "Sorry about that, girls. Everybody who has an overdue library book, please note the sign on the media center door that says to return them at once for inventory. If you can't read you are probably excused from —"

The intercom went dead again.

"And the final announcement is that the Cruisers will meet in Mr. Culpepper's office at the end of the last period. Anyone who doesn't show up will be burned at the stake. And have a nice day!"

"Yo, Zander, you going to show?" Kambui met me in the hallway.

"We have to show, I guess, but we need to work out a strategy for LaShonda," I said.

"Okay, you're in charge of the strategy," Kambui said.

"You couldn't think of anything, either?" I asked.

"LaShonda said she was just going to say no and walk away from the whole deal because she doesn't want her business all out there in the street," Kambui said. "And she definitely doesn't want it bouncing around Mr. C.'s office."

Mr. C. was smart, but as far as kids were concerned he was kind of lame at times. He kept talking about some perfect world and how all we had to do was to follow his road map and we would all get to heaven, make big bucks, and cop some Nobel prizes. When you didn't follow his program he got pissed and crawled down the back of your neck about what didn't you understand? What he didn't understand was that sometimes the world didn't work according to his logic. You can jump on a scholarship if you're jumping by yourself, but if you have a little brother to take care of, as LaShonda did, things get hard in a hurry.

What LaShonda was thinking was that if she never got to college she would have a hard time even supporting her brother once they aged out of the group home. I was feeling her strong.

Three times a week we have Phys Ed, which means forty-two minutes of hopping around and doing fake push-ups or doing lame exercises on the horse twice a week and one day of just jiving around. Nobody was going to the Olympics and nobody at Da Vinci was being recruited for big college sports except, and only maybe, Cody Weinstein could make a college team if he went Ivy League and changed his mind about playing basketball. His father was athletic director and kept pushing him to play, but they didn't get along very well. This was our jiving around day, and me, Kambui, Cody, and Alvin played H-O-R-S-E.

I could beat anybody at H-O-R-S-E any day of the week except for Cody, and sometimes I could beat him. Kambui couldn't play because he was too busy getting fancy with his short little arms, and he never made any of his shots.

"I talked to LaShonda," Kambui said. "And she said she wasn't going for the Virginia Woolf program and she wasn't going for the perfume company, either. She said she was just going to lay it out to Culpepper and school him on the happenings. Case closed."

I went to the corner and threw a jumper that swished cleanly through the net. It looked so pretty I wished I had it on tape. Kambui missed it, so did Alvin, but Cody made it.

The thing was that I knew it was never simply "case closed" when you were dealing with Culpepper. He was going to run down *this* and throw in some *that* and sprinkle in *obvious* a few times and remind everybody that he was an adult and in charge and we were just kids. LaShonda was right. She had to tell Mr. C. she had made up her mind and the case was closed and she didn't want to hear any more about it. It wasn't good but it was the only way to handle Mr. C.

"You think that Mr. C. is just going to let it slide?" I asked after I had whipped everybody.

"He doesn't have a choice," Kambui said.

"The thing with adults is that they don't know when they don't have a choice," Cody said. He had been listening to me and Kambui talk and we had filled him in. "You just wait and see."

The Cruisers met outside Mr. Culpepper's office and it was Bobbi who came up with the first cool observation.

"Why are we all here?" she asked.

"Because the announcement said we all had to be here," Kambui said. "And we already did our no-show bit yesterday."

"But why are we *all* here when it's only LaShonda's decision?" Bobbi went on. "He's got to be thinking about using us to put pressure on LaShonda. He's going to threaten us with something if we don't go along."

"What's he going to threaten us with?" LaShonda's voice went up. "He's not giving us anything."

"I don't know, either," Bobbi said. "But look out for Culpepper, he's sneaky."

"Hi, guys!" Caren Culpepper came out of her father's office and waved.

"Maybe he's going to get Caren to try out her charms on Zander again," LaShonda said, smiling.

I was glad to see her smiling.

We went in and sat on the bench in the waiting area. Mrs. Williams, the official Da Vinci secretary, looked up and smiled at us. We waited silently for about two minutes and then Kambui spoke up.

"He's probably watching us on closed-circuit television," he said. "I saw that once on *The First 48*. They were watching to see how nervous this dude was before they interrogated him."

"Did he confess?" Bobbi asked.

"Yes, but we haven't done anything," LaShonda said. "So all I'm going to say is the truth, and the truth is that I don't want any part of their program."

Mr. Culpepper came to his office door, twisted his face into a kind of smile, and then beckoned us all in. I was confident. I glanced over at LaShonda and she had her battle face on.

We went in and sat down and I saw that Bobbi had her battle face on, too.

"LaShonda, I really respect your decision," Mr. Culpepper started. "I fully understand how much your brother means to you and what a sacrifice it will be for both of you to turn down this opportunity. But that's what life is about, taking the road we see that best fits our needs. I know your friends have been supportive and will continue to be. I've asked you all here today simply to consider the problem as presented to me by St. Francis."

"I don't care what they say." LaShonda was getting mad.

"I care because I see so much talent in you young people," Mr. Culpepper said. "I can't wait to see the play again just to see your costumes."

"I don't want them to wear my costumes again," LaShonda said. "As far as I'm concerned, they can go on naked."

"You can't do that, LaShonda Powell!" Mr. Culpepper was already turning a fifth shade of red. "There will be NO nudity involved with any students from Da Vinci!"

"Then you better cancel the whole performance!" LaShonda was getting up close and personal, and Kambui was trying to get in between them.

"This is . . . this is . . . the chance of a lifetime, young lady." Our assistant principal was beginning to sputter, and Kambui was practically dragging LaShonda out of the door.

Bobbi McCall was in tears. Yes, tough-as-nails Bobbi was on the verge of a major boo-hoo.

"What's going on?" I asked Bobbi in the hallway. "I thought LaShonda was doing great."

"She was," Bobbi said. "Until they told her that if she took the scholarship they would have to separate her from her brother. No way she's doing that, Zander. And the Cruisers have to back her up!"

I knew the play we were going to put on again would put the Cruisers on the map big-time, especially with all the noise about LaShonda's costumes. But if we blew it after all the press coverage they wouldn't be able to dig a hole deep enough for us to crawl in!

I was getting nervous.

"What did St. Francis say?" Kambui asked.

I had a sinking feeling.

"What they said was that they didn't see how I was going to support my brother once I aged out of St. Francis," LaShonda said. "There will have to be —"

LaShonda was already crying.

"Yo, LaShonda, you got any ideas about — you know — what other people do in, like, your situation?" Kambui said.

"If they're rich they can hire somebody full-time," LaShonda said. "Other than that it depends on how people — the children — are getting on. If they're like Chris there comes a time when . . . you have to make a decision to walk away or — I don't know. I just don't know!"

I hate to see a friend cry. I was blinking back tears and feeling sick to my stomach. It just wasn't fair, and it wasn't fair right out there in the open where we could all see it.

We all hugged LaShonda before she left, her books clutched to her chest, her head down, going toward the boulevard.

"If I die and come back to life I'm coming as a frog!" Bobbi said. "Then all I'd have to do is swim around in muddy water and burp, or whatever the heck frogs do."

THE CRUISER

POEM TO MY BROTHER

By LaShonda Powell

There will always be summer rains

Leaves glistening in the sun

Weighed down by golden droplets

Beautiful in their silence

As there will always be us

    There will always be birds

    Singing morning hymns in

    Distant forests

    Though no one will hear

    As there will always be us

There will always be mountains

Booming their majesty

To the open arms of the sky

Summer rain, birds, mountains

As there will always be us

CHAPTER FIVE

To Be or Not to Be

"Yo, Zander." Kambui and I were going up the hill on the way to school. "If it was scientifically proven that roaches were the perfect food, and you lived an extra year for every thousand roaches you ate, how many would you eat?"

"The question is stupid and I'm not answering any stupid questions today," I said.

"It's not stupid," he said. "You're just too intellectually lazy to get to it."

"None. I'd kill myself by not eating roaches," I said.

"That makes sense to you?" Kambui asked. "You could grow them for free and save on your grocery bills and everything. I'd eat every roach I saw."

"Check out the television truck in front of the school," I

said. There was one of those vans with the round antennas parked in front of Da Vinci.

"You might as well stop eating today," Kambui went on. "If eating doesn't mean good health to you, then what are you eating for? You say you don't eat junk food, right?"

"What I'm going to do is watch you eat up all the roaches and then make a fortune writing about you," I said. "I'll die young, but at least my breath won't smell like roaches."

"That looks like some kind of a demonstration," Kambui said. "Check out those folks carrying signs."

"They've probably heard we're over here eating roaches," I said as I checked out the signs.

COMPLETE! NOT ELITE!
All Students Are Created Equal!

"What are they talking about?" I wondered aloud.

"I don't know," Kambui answered.

As we neared the school I saw Bobbi McCall, and we walked toward her. She was on her cell phone.

"Zander, Mrs. Maxwell wants the Cruisers in her office right away," Bobbi said. She was wearing feathers in her hair that went all the way around her head. It looked good.

"What did we do now?" Kambui asked.

I couldn't think of anything the Cruisers had done or even had published in our paper. But Mrs. Maxwell was cool and everybody knew that, so I wasn't sweating it.

The people carrying signs were also chanting something, but I couldn't understand what they were saying and it didn't seem like a really big deal to me because somebody in Harlem was always protesting something.

Me, Kambui, and Bobbi went in the front door of Da Vinci and Mrs. Brown, who works in Mrs. Maxwell's office, motioned to us to come up the steps. On the way up Bobbi said she thought it was about our agreeing in *The Cruiser* to referee a food fight. Actually, we were just kidding, but maybe Mrs. Maxwell had taken it seriously.

"I think it's about the protest," Mrs. Brown said.

We got to the principal's office and it was already crowded. There was a woman with a voice recorder who I figured was a reporter. LaShonda, looking tired, was already there. She kind of half smiled at us and shrugged. She didn't know anything, either.

"How you doing?" I asked LaShonda.

"Hanging in there," she said. "I don't think this has anything to do with us."

Mrs. Brown motioned the Cruisers and the reporter lady into the principal's office and we filed in. Mrs. Maxwell was standing behind her desk. Mr. Culpepper was standing in front of the American flag next to one of the school's security guards, and on the other side was a dude dressed in an African robe and another guy I recognized. I had seen Charles Lord on television and in the *Amsterdam News* a lot of times. He was one of those dudes who was always against whatever was going on and always making statements to the papers.

"Mrs. Maxwell, I'm going to say again that I do not approve of these children being here," Mr. Lord said. "This is a matter for adults to decide."

"It's their future you're challenging, Mr. Lord." Mrs. Maxwell's voice was a little strained and I figured she was upset. "You cannot be against elite schools without being against elite pupils such as these young people. So you have to make your case to them!"

"Are these students among the school's best?" the reporter asked.

"These students are just young people who work very hard to do well in the educational system," Mrs. Maxwell said. "And who, *apparently*, Mr. Lord is against."

"My case is very simple." Mr. Lord turned toward where the Cruisers stood on one side of the room. "I don't think that there should be elite schools such as this one in the city of New York. I think that all students should have the opportunities that you have here. And that's regardless of race, color, religion, or economic status. I hope you young people can agree with me and the Harlem community in this matter."

"My grandmother saw you on television," Kambui said. "She said people like you don't build anything, you just tear stuff down."

"Your grandmother is correct, young man," Mr. Lord said. "It's up to the city to build a competent educational system for all the children in New York. It's up to people like me to tear down their excuses, one of which is the city's elite schools, for not building a complete educational system for all the students in the city."

That was a good answer and it was really fast.

"You're quick and slick," I said. "But being strong

doesn't mean you're not wrong. Da Vinci is the bomb because everybody here works hard. If the really good schools in the city are smoking it's because the kids who go to them aren't joking. Wrap that up and send it to your brain."

"'Nuff said, Zander man!" This from Bobbi.

I looked at Mr. Lord and I could see he was thinking big-time but wasn't coming up with anything.

"That was a very intelligent remark and I appreciate it," Mr. Lord said. He had turned away from the Cruisers and Mrs. Maxwell and was talking to the reporter. "But I don't think you children can understand the complexities of the fight for black education that I've been involved with over the years. I have been in the forefront of trying to get our people —"

Bobbi started out the door and the rest of the Cruisers followed her. We knew we had smoked Mr. Lord and he knew it, too. When adults start calling you "children" and start hanging stuff like "complexity" on you, then it's clear that they can't think of anything better to say.

The thing was that a lot of people, and especially Charles Lord, had been taking shots at Da Vinci. They wanted to point out how many kids in public schools were doing badly, but they had turned the whole deal around so that it looked like it was the fault of the schools that were doing well. I could dig where they were coming from but I also knew that the students at Da Vinci were expected to do more work than kids in most schools. And we were doing it. Case closed. Even the Cruisers, who weren't all rah-rah about good grades, knew we had to represent.

Bobbi had to go to Phys Ed and Kambui went to the media center to look up something, and so when LaShonda caught up with me and took my arm we were alone, except for three hundred other kids going through the hallway.

"Zander man, thanks for your support," LaShonda said. "I really appreciate it."

"You need me, just call me," I said, rather heroically.

"I'd marry you if you weren't already hooked up with Caren," LaShonda said, her smile spreading across her face.

"Hey, I'm not hooked up with Caren Culpepper!" I said.

"Of course you're not," LaShonda said, all wide-eyed like she knew I didn't believe what she was saying.

"LaShonda —"

"It's all platonic, right?" she asked.

THE CRUISER

MY READING LIST

By Bobbi McCall

1. *Speak* by Laurie Halse Anderson

2. *Rebecca* by Daphne du Maurier

3. *The Diary of a Young Girl* by Anne Frank

4. *A Wizard of Earthsea* by Ursula K. Le Guin

5. *After the Rain* by Norma Fox Mazer

6. *Define "Normal"* by Julie Anne Peters

7. *Island of the Blue Dolphins* by Scott O'Dell

8. *Holes* by Louis Sachar

9. *Platero and I* by Juan Ramón Jiménez

10. *The Gay Genius: The Life and Times of Su Tungpo* by Lin Yutang

Uh-oh, too many books for the kids at Saltine Middle School? I'll drop the last four.

Uh-oh, too hard for the kids at Oreo Academy? I'll drop *Rebecca* and *A Wizard of Earthsea*.

Uh-oh, interferes with Silent TV, Wednesdays at the Vanilla Wafer School? I'll drop Anne Frank and *After the Rain*.

Uh-oh, they've run out of Cliff Notes for *Define "Normal"*? I'll drop it.

That just leaves *Speak*, but now I guess we've achieved equal opportunity — at least in reading. And, oh, yes, we're dropping all math that has an equation with an x or any other unknown.

THE CRUISER

MOUNTAINS

By Zander Scott

Some people climb mountains for the sheer joy of accepting a challenge. Mr. Lord thinks we should stop these people at once because others don't see mountain climbing as a joyful experience. Or education, either.

Some people climb mountains because their

parents climbed them, and they think it's normal to climb. Mr. Lord thinks we should definitely stop these people to get back at the parents.

Some people climb mountains because the extra effort doesn't bother them. Mr. Lord thinks we shouldn't have mountain climbing until it becomes easy, maybe with escalators.

Some people, Mr. Lord, see the rewards on the tops of the mountains and understand that those rewards will make life better for them. And some people, Mr. Lord, are struggling with burdens you can't even imagine, and they struggle up the mountain hoping to find a life that they, and the people they love, can call normal.

For some people, Mr. Lord, it is only the view from the mountaintop that will make us whole.

CHAPTER SIX

Frailty, Thy Name Is Not Sagal

All Cruisers! All Cruisers! Get over to FDA NOW! They're saying
that Sagal can't run the dash unless she strips down to shorts!
Bring guns and ammo! — BOBBI MAC

I had been thinking of going over to Frederick Douglass
Academy to show the Da Vinci girls' track team some love
but I got myself sidetracked thinking about LaShonda's
problem. The thing was that I always thought that if you
had a problem all you had to do was be smart enough and
you could solve it. Now I was running into problems that
looked as if it didn't matter if you were smart because they
didn't have any good solutions.

LaShonda's problem was real and I didn't see a solution
to it. I could figure out what to do — if she didn't want to
be separated from her brother then she should stick to her

game plan. That was all cool but it didn't make things right because they were still poor and he was still needing her.

When I got Bobbi's text message I knew what that was about and I almost felt as if I didn't want to go over to FDA. FDA kids thought they were so smart — most of them were — but they were constantly scoping out Da Vinci for a beat down. Everybody in the school leagues knew that Sagal, the anchor on the Da Vinci girls' relay team, was a Muslim and couldn't strip down to shorts, but nobody made an issue of it until they found out just how fast she was. The girl could run!

Kambui comes up with a lot of lame sayings but when he talked about Sagal I thought maybe he had something going on. I met him in the train station at 148th Street and we walked toward FDA together.

"Sagal will fight them if they try to stop her from running," Kambui said. He had his camera out and was filming everything. "And if she fights, I'm going to fight with her, man!"

Yeah, right.

Sagal Shehabi was born in Kandahar, Afghanistan. Her father made a living as an appliance repairman and her mother baked bread and sold it. Sagal was wounded in the fighting between Americans and the Taliban and to prove it had a really ugly scar that ran across her forehead, down alongside her nose, and across the tip of her chin. She was usually quiet and stayed to herself and you would have thought that she didn't know anything. But her grades were good and she tried to blend in with the American girls. When she went out for the track team the other girls thought she didn't understand what it meant because she showed up in loose-fitting pants and wore a *hijab*, which covered her hair. But when she ran they knew she had something serious going on.

So me and Kambui showed our IDs downstairs and went up to FDA's gym.

"Yo, Zander, you getting uglier!" I recognized Freddy Brandt sitting in the bleachers. He was in FDA's band. "You looking like a sissy King Kong!"

"And I can smell your breath from here!" I called back. "You need to stop rinsing your false teeth in the toilet bowl."

Mr. Weinstein, our athletic director, was on the gym floor talking to the FDA coach when I got over to them.

"Zander, go sit down!" Mr. Weinstein said.

"I'm here to —"

"Go sit down!" he yelled.

I gave him a look, but I didn't hold it too long because I really didn't think he was wrapped too tight and he was built like he could knock you out with one punch.

Bobbi found me and started running the whole set down in fast-forward time.

"They're *talking* about how everyone has to wear the same uniform, but I think it's just because they don't want their precious darlings to get beat and they don't even have the fastest girls in this school on the team because they need a 'cute' factor and our girls don't play cute!"

I knew Bobbi was coming from a feminist position and everything because she lived with two women, but our girls, except for Sagal, were just *too* cute, especially on the relay team. We had the Hopkins sisters, Shantese and Zhade, both of whom I would die for, Maria Torres, who could fly and was fly, and Sagal bringing it home.

Dr. Barnwell, FDA's principal, came out on the floor and called the FDA coach and Mr. Weinstein over. They had a meeting in the middle of the floor and you could tell by Mr. Weinstein's body language that things were not going good for Da Vinci.

Finally, the FDA coach got on the loudspeaker and made an announcement that the Da Vinci relay team had withdrawn. All the FDA kids started hooting at us.

But then . . .

But then Sagal went to the center of the floor and took the mike from the FDA coach's hand and spoke into it.

"We are withdrawing from the race because you Americans are afraid to compete against a Muslim girl. If your girls can't run fast I can understand that. I feel sorry for you."

She handed the mike back to the FDA coach and walked away.

All the FDA students started yelling and saying how they would run away from us and we weren't this and we weren't that. Well, what that did was to get all the school officials back onto the middle of the floor with their heads together.

"We have to get Sagal into the Cruisers," I said to Bobbi.

"Her parents are too strict," Bobbi said. "They won't let her join. The only reason she's on the track team is that she ran with her brothers in Afghanistan."

Body language. Mr. Weinstein started toward us and beckoned toward the girls. They were going to run.

There were four teams in the relay: FDA as the host school, Wadleigh, Arts and Sciences, and Da Vinci. I thought our girls could beat FDA but I knew that Wadleigh was just plain tough and you could never tell about a team from Arts and Sciences. Sometimes they would show up ready and sometimes they would be jiving around.

The race was four by a hundred, which meant that each girl would run one hundred yards and then pass the baton on to the next girl. The biggest danger was falling too far behind and then getting careless with the baton. You only had a small area in which you could pass the baton, and if you dropped it you were just out of luck. The race would be over before you picked it up.

Shantese was down in the starting blocks and she looked ready. She was wearing really short running pants and her stomach was bare.

"Yo, Zander, push your eyes back in their sockets," Bobbi said. "You're embarrassing the school!"

Down the track, Zhade was waiting with the other girls who were going to run the second leg. Maria Torres was straight across from me. On the far side, to my left, I could see Sagal. She was wearing a green *hijood* that covered her hair and neck. Her arms were covered down to her wrists and her legs were covered down to the tops of her running shoes. The girls from the other teams around her were running their mouths.

Body language.

"Yo, Kambui, check out that scene," I said. "They're trying to intimidate Sagal."

"You think we should go over there and stare them down?" Kambui asked.

"Don't bother." Bobbi was leaning against Kambui. "She's been wounded in her body and face, shot at by the Taliban, and she's still got the nerve to compete. They're not making her nervous."

The gun went off and the race was on. Shantese got a late start and was behind the other girls as she rounded the first turn. The girl from Wadleigh, very short and very dark, was smooth on the front end and she looked like she could have done the whole race by herself. I watched the girls in the second leg line up. I glanced at the clock. The girl from Wadleigh passed the baton a hair past eleven seconds.

If Zhade asked me to marry her I would probably say yes, even though I didn't have a job or anything. And she could run. She started off five yards behind the other girls but made up half the distance by the time she reached Maria.

I could see Maria digging down and leaning on the curve. She was looking great and quickly passed one of the girls. When she hit the far curve she was stride for stride with the second girl. Maybe just a body length behind.

Sometimes the fastest runner is the anchor and sometimes the positions are just about who can handle running on a curve best. When Maria reached out the baton to Sagal my heart was in my mouth. Then Maria fell!

"Crap!" Bobbi said.

"She passed it!" Kambui came back. "Sagal's got the baton!"

I saw Sagal switch the baton from her left hand to her right. Her legs were pumping like crazy as she leaned into the last turn and headed for the last sixty yards. She was still a yard behind the leader, a big, powerful-looking girl wearing the blue and white Wadleigh uniform.

"Run, Sagal, run!" Bobbi was screaming.

Sagal was running hard and I couldn't tell who was in front. Then I saw the girl from Wadleigh's hands go up as they crossed the finish line.

"Who got it? Who got it?" Mr. Weinstein was pushing me with one hand and looking toward the officials.

The two officials put their heads together for a moment and then one of them made a motion, bringing his finger around his head. The girl with her head covered had won!

Yes!

Okay, so Sagal wasn't the best-looking girl in the school and her face was scarred, but right then and there I would have married her, too.

THE PALETTE

WHAT I LOVE ABOUT AMERICA
By Sergeant Olga Litowinsky

I was told that the Cruisers all showed up in support of Sagal Shehabi at the track meet at FDA. Sagal helped Da Vinci win the race she was in and helped the entire athletic squad win the meet. Although it was a personal victory for those who experienced it, what appealed to me was that Americans are always willing to let everyone compete. I congratulate Da Vinci, Sagal, the track team, and the Cruisers.

I have just served my third tour in the Middle East and I think I see a lot of progress as the area stabilizes. Sometimes the day-to-day operations are hectic, but I know American troops, especially those in Civilian Relations, are doing their best to bring peace to the country. I have had a few narrow escapes and have had to fire my weapon on occasion, but I am proud to be an American and proud of what we have done in this troubled part of the world.

The question I am going to ask you when this film is finished" — Mr. Siegfried pushed his glasses up on his nose — "is how many people, in how many countries, make a profit from this one simple operation of manufacturing chocolate? Yes, you might take out your notebooks and do the calculations, but you will not talk during this short film."

"Would you mind if I ran out and got some popcorn?" Phat Tony asked.

Mr. Siegfried walked over to Phat Tony's desk. "Mr. Williams, may I share with you two small facts? The first is that you are far less amusing than you imagine you are, and the second is that you are on the very cusp of failing Social Studies. I derive a great deal of pleasure in failing students who overestimate their cleverness. Shall we continue with your supposedly witty remarks or shall we discard our humor for the time being, sir?"

"We can let it go, sir," Phat Tony said, slumping down into his seat.

The room didn't really get dark but we could see the film all right. First they showed this family sitting around the table having cups of cocoa in the morning and then this voice-over came on asking if anybody wondered how this "delicious cup of goodness" got to their breakfast table.

One boy said that they made it in New Jersey, but I didn't believe that.

Then we saw the woman in the family buying the cocoa in the supermarket, then there was a picture of a black guy driving boxes of the stuff from a warehouse. I put down some tick marks on a sheet of paper. After that there was a ship with huge steel containers of something I assumed was cocoa and then a quick shot of people loading the ship.

"I'm giving this film one and a half stars," Kambui said.

Then the film showed a farm and trees and stuff. I didn't know cocoa grew on trees, so that was kind of interesting. We watched people gathering the plants and loading them onto trucks. Some of them were looking at the camera and smiling and I liked that.

When the film ended everybody started comparing their number of how many people made money on the cocoa. I had counted five: the guy who ran the supermarket, the guy who brought the cocoa from the warehouse to the supermarket, whoever brought it to the warehouse from the ship, whoever brought it to the ship, and whoever grew it in the first place.

With Mr. Siegfried you were always going to be wrong. He was fair on tests, but in class he had a way of always making you feel off balance.

He started adding in bookkeepers, the people who made the containers, salespeople, and even people who traded in cocoa on the stock exchange. Boring. I could see where Mr. Siegfried was coming from but I really didn't care.

"There were children picking the cocoa," Bobbi said. "How come they weren't in school? The announcer said it was their winter."

I thought that Mr. Siegfried was going to say something about kids going to school wasn't our subject, but he didn't.

He got right on Bobbi's comments and asked her to look up when the schools were open in Brazil, where the film had been made.

"And I'll give you extra credit if you document your findings, Miss McCall."

That was swift of Bobbi, but I felt a little bad that I hadn't picked up on it. The thing was that Bobbi picked up on a lot of things that other people didn't.

The afternoon went by and I kind of vegged out. I saw LaShonda across the hall and she signaled a *T* for me to text her.

what's up?

wanna come to a tennis game this afternoon?

u playing?

no, Chris is. it's an xhibition at Jackie Robinson Park.

yeah, ok — what time?

3:30

see ya then

I didn't know what kind of program it was going to be but I thought I would go just to show LaShonda some support. I had seen handicapped kids play sports before and didn't really dig it. It was good that Chris was getting out more, though.

The thing was I didn't know what was actually wrong with Chris but I knew something wasn't right. Whenever I saw him and LaShonda was around he would put his forehead against her and keep it there unless they needed to walk somewhere. He was a friendly kid, sort of, but he never looked right at you. It was like he was overhearing a conversation rather than you were talking to him.

I went right from school to the park. I asked Kambui to come with me but he had to take his grandmother to the Social Security office. I got to the park just at three-thirty and there weren't many kids there. In the swing section there were some women with small kids and one fat lady with some rabbits and a serious little girl trying to get the rabbits to sit together.

LaShonda was sitting on a bench facing the basketball court and I joined her.

"What's going on?" I asked.

"Just needed somebody to holler at," she said. "See how the words sound when they come out of my mouth."

"I know it's hard," I said.

"Do you?" LaShonda turned and looked at me.

"Yeah."

"Look, here come the kids to play tennis," she said. "Watch Chris play."

I didn't know any of the six kids, all about nine or ten, on the tennis court and I figured they must have all been from St. Francis. A bald-headed dude who was running things separated them into two groups of three and put them on different sides of the two nets. The kids on the right side were setting up a doubles match, and Baldy placed one near the net and the other one farther back. He tossed the ball over the net and the kids on the other side both ran to it and started swinging. They missed the ball, ran and got it, and tossed it back to Baldy. Then they went through the whole process again. They did it three times before the kids even hit the ball once. But after a while they would get the ball and throw it over the net, which seemed okay with them.

Baldy went on one side of the other net, away from Chris, then served the ball to him.

Chris Powell got to the ball in a heartbeat and pounded

it over the net. Baldy got to it and lobbed it high. Chris let it bounce and then slammed it over again, past Baldy who was lunging for it.

"Yo, he can play," I said.

"If he knows I'm here he can play, or do almost anything," LaShonda said. "If he takes his meds he's right in the game."

"The tennis game?" I asked. "He's, like, really into tennis?"

LaShonda didn't answer at first and I turned back toward where Baldy was hitting the ball with Chris. Once in a while the ball would come to the other kid who would try to get it over the net, but it was Chris who was the athlete. I kept thinking of when LaShonda played basketball in the gym. She was ferocious and quick and I knew she would have been great on the school's girls' team, but she'd never gone out for it.

Meanwhile on the court, Chris kept getting to the ball and kept hitting it back across the net. But every once in a while he would look over to where me and LaShonda were sitting and I could feel he needed to have her there.

"When we were with my parents, my dad used to beat on my mom all the time," LaShonda said. "He was so violent she had to go to the hospital at least once a month. He got locked up once or twice but when he got out she would let him back home. Then one day he was beating on her and I tried to get in between them."

"What happened?"

"I don't even know." LaShonda smiled for a brief second and let it die. "I guess he hit me and knocked me out. When I came back around there was blood all over the place. She cleaned up everything before she took me to the hospital. I had nerve damage or something, I don't know. I got over it, though. Eventually, he got involved in some street fight and cut a dude and got some prison time. When he got out the last time he didn't even come around, but once in a while he would see my mother on the street and threaten her.

"She got messed around and started drinking and couldn't control that, and they took us out of the house. She got arrested now and then for whatever she was doing in her life and we've been at St. Francis ever since."

"Your father hit Chris, too?"

"No, he beat my mother up, and sometimes he would slap me around," LaShonda said. "But he never hit Chris."

"So, how come . . . you know?"

"The doctor said that Chris seeing all that violence, and being in the house with it and having it happen to people he was close to, was just about the same as him being hit. That's just the way it is. I'm what he's got, Zander. And he's what I got."

I watched Chris hit the ball, watched him move around the court and glance over to where LaShonda sat with me. Whenever he looked our way, she smiled.

THE CRUISER

A POEM THAT'S NOT A POEM

By Bobbi McCall and Zander Scott

This is a poem that's not

A poem, but an enjambment session full

Of similes and strange words that

Come like yesterday's news

Pretending to be history when

They know they are not history at all

But the story of a stranger

Living within his body

As some people are not

People but poems walking

In perfect irony

Pretending to be people

But we know that they are only

Sequences of our care for them

That flutter like butterflies

Around the heart

This is a poem

That is not a poem

As there are people

Who are not people

But with enough love

They come close enough

CHAPTER EIGHT

Put Money in Thy Purse

What happened last Thursday, conversation past.

Four o'clock in the afternoon, which is like one o'clock West Coast time, and things start popping off. First, the home phone rings and that means it's either a bill collector, a junk call, or my father. Mom answers it and collapses into her lotus position. I can't do that but she hits it like it's nothing. Her knees bend out and she goes down in one motion. Very cool.

When her eyes roll up I know it's Donald Scott, famous weatherman and long-distance father. Mom switched the phone to speaker.

"You're public," she said.

"So, how are things going?"

"Wonderful, I just got the Nobel prize for being sexy."

"I guess 'serious' is still not in your repertoire. How's Zander?"

"Zander, how are you?"

"Wonderful."

"What have you two been up to?"

"I'm up to five foot nine, and Zander's up to six feet."

"I mean, what have you been doing?"

"We're planning a major robbery. Zander found an abandoned time machine and we're going to use it to steal next weekend and sell it to the Iranians. What do you think?"

"What I think is that your sorry attempts at humor are not at all funny. I am concerned with my son's well-being and I would appreciate it if you would not treat my phone calls lightly!"

"You're not going to rat us out, are you?"

"May I speak to Zander?"

"Zander?"

"Yo!"

"So, how are things going?"

"All right."

"And school?"

"All right."

"I wanted to talk to you about an allowance. A boy your age needs to have a sense of responsibility about money. I was reading an article recently suggesting that fiscal stability often starts in one's teenage years. (Mom is frantically writing a note.) *If you learn how to manage money in your teen years you'll probably retire in good condition."*

"So how much we talking about?"

"I want you to spend a few days thinking about the amount and then call me back with the amount and with a rationalization for that amount. Can you do that?"

"Yeah."

"Fine, and Zander, I want this to be from you and nobody else. And I want you to be serious. Can I count on you?"

"Yeah."

"Okay, I'll wait to hear from you. And say good-bye to your mother for me."

"Hey, Dad, can I ask you something?"

"Of course."

"You know, I have a friend, LaShonda, who's worried about what's going to happen to her and her brother in a few years. They're living in a group home. You know what that is?"

"Yes, of course. It's one of those places that children who are without parents live."

"Or their parents can't deal with them. Anyway, she's only fourteen now but she says when she reaches eighteen she could age out. That means they only get funding for kids under eighteen."

"I've heard about that."

"Well, that kind of sucks, and I thought that if a lot of people knew about it — you know — if you got it on television then maybe we could get the rules changed so that —"

"It's been done."

"What?"

"It's been done. There was a program aired about . . . two, maybe three years ago on the topic. They never repeat the feature story — and that's what that would be, a feature — within a three-year period."

"What's that mean?"

"It means that if they air a story they won't air the same story again unless there's a dramatic new twist to it. It just won't fly."

"But it's still happening."

"*So you'll get back to me on the allowance, Zander. And remember, I respect your maturity and I look forward to a man-to-man conversation.*"

"Yeah."

All kinds of sadness started going on. Mom was crying, which she does after about half of my father's phone calls, and I was mad, which I am after half his phone calls, and a whole bunch of things weren't making any sense. We were taking Algebra in school and figuring out what x was or what y was and jumping all over the unknowns like they were lame and we just had to track their little unknown butts down. Once we tracked them down ($x = y+2$), the problem was solved. But in real life you could track down whatever x or y was and nothing was solved. Everybody knew about kids getting aged out, but nobody was going any further. My father even changed the problem from kids aging out to what would make a good television program.

Mom was down with the problem but after the phone call from the Friendly Weatherman she was all about what was bruising her cruising.

"I think that he thinks that if he gives you a fat allowance then you simply won't need me anymore," she said.

"He's always thinking something" was my lame answer.

I couldn't really feel their fights because I couldn't see a reason for them. Pops had split, moved out to the West Coast, got a new wife and another kid (nasty little girl!), while Mom and me had stayed in Harlem and kept on keeping on. But if there was going to be a fight then I was on Mom's side because she was my heart and he was, like, *in the wind*. Case closed.

"He asked what we were doing and I couldn't think of anything!" she said.

"You don't have to prove anything to him," I said.

"I still feel bad," Mom said. "We have to do more things together."

That smelled like trouble. But it didn't get to be real trouble until Monday.

"I ordered a cassoulet kit," Mom said, smiling. It was the same smile she used for toothpaste commercials. "Do you know what that is?"

"Something that women use to clean their private parts?"

"Oh! Oh! No!"

Right away I guessed I was wrong.

THE CRUISER

OVERHEARD

By A. Nanny Moose

FOUR MINUTES TO AIRTIME:

HOTSHOT PRESENTER RONALD POTT

Okay, okay! What do we have?

REPORTER ONE

We have a fire in Seattle. A two-story —

HPRP

It's been done. What else?

REPORTER TWO

A black kid was shot on —

HPRP

Same old, same old. What else?

REPORTER TWO

This kid was an honor student at —

HPRP

Yeah, yeah. It's been done.

REPORTER THREE

Tsunami in Southeast Asia. Hundreds killed!

HPRP

If it happens in England it's news. What else?
Come on, people, give me something!

REPORTER ONE

A corruption indictment in Jersey City! Two
prominent politicians indicted!

HPRP

It's been done! It's been done!

ONE MINUTE TO AIRTIME:

REPORTER TWO

A jailbreak in Crown Point, Indiana.

HPRP

Who cares? C'mon! C'mon!

A nuclear meltdown in India! It could be the end of the world!

HPRP

Not sexy enough. What else you got?

FIVE SECONDS TO AIRTIME:

REPORTER TWO

Lindsay Lohan got arrested again. For shoplifting!

WE'RE ON!

HPRP

Good evening, America! I'm sad to report tonight that Paris Hilton is deeply depressed over the arrest of her friend Lindsay Lohan on what appear to be trumped-up charges. WPOP has an exclusive interview with Ms. Hilton.

MS. HILTON

I am deeply depressed over the arrest of my friend Lindsay Lohan on what appear to be trumped-up charges. I can't say anything more at this time as I am much too emotional.

CHAPTER NINE
Soak Them Beans!

Sunday night, and the whole world fell apart. I was watching *Night of the Dancing Zombies* in HD on the television and the same movie on my netbook in Korean. They came on at the same time but the television version was ahead of the netbook version and I was trying to warn the dudes on netbook what was about to go down. It was like I could see into the future (about six seconds into the future) and come almost close to ruling the world. Then Mrs. Jones called and told Mom that Mr. Lord was on television bad-mouthing Da Vinci. Mom switched channels (without saying anything to me, which she would have been pissed if I had done!) and I saw Lord running his mouth as usual.

"If they are supposed to be specially gifted, what are they doing for the community with their alleged gifts?"

He was about an inch away from the camera. "I don't see anything that they are accomplishing!"

Then there was a cut to the time we were all in Mrs. Maxwell's office and I saw the Cruisers standing there. On-screen my head looked like a giant cantaloupe with braids. The only voice that was heard on the tape was Mr. Lord's, and he looked like he was getting madder every moment.

As soon as the news clip ended the telephone started ringing. Jody called, Kambui got on the horn, Kelly Bena, LaShonda, and then Mrs. Maxwell.

"I spoke to a reporter this afternoon but I wouldn't allow myself to be photographed," she said in that cool, calm voice she has. "I told them that one thing we had in mind to do for the community would be to present a play in the school auditorium. I did mention an evening performance a week from this coming Thursday. I hope that sits well with the Cruisers."

Yo! She called us the Cruisers. That sat well with me already. It meant we were getting props from our main lady. But then I thought about what play she was talking about and I knew it was *Act Six* and I wondered if LaShonda was going to go for it. She had done the costumes and I wanted them to be used in the play really bad. In the first place I looked good in mine, and in the second place I wanted LaShonda to get over it. She was really an angel and she needed to get her glow on despite what bad things came her way. I believed that. Truly. Mom and me had been living it even though we weren't always talking it. We were always going for the glow and hoping for the best.

"I can't speak for all of the Cruisers tonight," I said to Mrs. Maxwell, "but I'm going for it big-time and I think they will, too."

I called Bobbi and told her what the deal was.

"I'll set up a conference call and we can discuss it," she said.

"Are you down for it?" I asked.

"If we put on the play for the community we might get some television coverage," Bobbi said. "If we get television coverage then we blow ourselves up and our argument gets louder. If it gets loud enough, maybe somebody will actually listen to us when we talk about LaShonda's situation and anything else we need to say."

"You thought of all that just now?"

"Yeah, what were you thinking?"

"How can you think that fast?"

"I'm a girl, we think faster than boys!"

"Whatever."

Bobbi set up the conference call and Kambui was down with putting on the play. LaShonda wasn't sure.

"I think I just want to lie low for a minute," she said. "Maybe go back to just being plain old LaShonda."

"You've got talent, girl," Bobbi said. "You can't walk away from that. It's going to stay with you, and you're either going to work it or it's going to eat at you until it messes you up."

"The Cruisers are behind me?" LaShonda asked.

"I'm here," Kambui said.

"I'm with you, girlfriend," Bobbi said.

"I'll lay it all down for you, LaShonda," I said. "For you and for your brother. Whatever it takes, I got your back."

"Okay," LaShonda said. "Let's do it."

After we hung up I put on the tube and stared at some reality jam. Only it wasn't really reality because it wasn't touching anything that I was feeling. I was happy and proud that the Cruisers showed strong for LaShonda, but I wasn't sure of myself. In the movies when a crew got together the background music started to play and they all got these cool looks on their faces and every-thing worked out fine. We were all still hoping things were going to work out and I was a little scared. Okay, a lot scared.

Also, how come Bobbi had got on top of things so fast? She had thought it out before I could even spit it out. I didn't know if girls could really think faster than boys, but that girl sure smoked me!

Okay. Woke up on a Tuesday morning and everything looked fine. My room was still rectangular, the windows were still in the same place, and there were still cars double-parked in the street below.

When I got out to the kitchen Mom was at the table pushing a piece of lemon around her teacup with the spoon.

"Why are you doing that?" I asked.

"Just thinking about what your father was saying the other day." Mom sounded moany. "I wonder if he thinks I'm a lousy parent?"

"What do you care?" I asked. "I think you're okay."

"You're just in love with my mac and cheese," she said.

"So today we're going to be doing the duck dish, right?" I said. "I even got Bobbi coming over to help and she's not into cooking."

"I hope it turns out all right," Mom said. "They said it was easy on the website."

Mom was sweating making a fancy dish with me. It was funny in a way and not funny at the same time. She was an adult and we had been doing okay most of the time, but here she was getting all nervous about making dinner.

I checked out my teeth and rinsed. Then I washed my face and checked out how big my head looked in the mirror. It was kind of big but not as big as it looked on television.

"You're going to come straight from school, right?" Mom at the door.

"Yeah. Hey, do you think I've got a big head?"

"It's kind of big," Mom said, turning my face toward her. "But you're good-looking, so it's okay. Good-looking covers up a lot of stuff."

"When do you think people will stop having problems?"

"You mean when will there be world peace and the end of poverty?" Mom asked.

"No, like, when do you stop worrying about how you're doing?" I said. "You said looking good covers up a lot of stuff, and you look great, but . . ."

"Some things you always worry about, I think," Mom said. "When I was young my mother used to dress me so I would look frumpy and the boys wouldn't notice me. She was always worried that some boy would take advantage of me. She still worries about it because people are people and they do what they want to do. And sometimes — well, you know. . . ."

"What?"

"They do what they need to do instead of what they should be doing," Mom said. "You've got things going on in your head that you know are right but you don't always follow those things. Sometimes you just do what makes you comfortable."

"Like making this duck thing?"

"It'll be cool if it turns out great, won't it?"

"And when Dad calls and says what are you doing we can say we were making a duck castle, or whatever."

"Cassoulet. Cass-oo-lay! It's French."

"It's a French duck?"

"It's a French recipe."

"Okay, we'll do it."

"So the point of the whole thing is that Mom is worried because my father's putting her down because we aren't running around living the high life," I said to Kambui. "So we're going to make this fancy French dish just so she can tell him about it."

"Yeah, but that's, like, a girl thing, right?" Kambui was texting as we walked.

"I think it's more a fancy thing than a girl thing," I said. "Anyway, Mom said that most of the top cooks in the world are guys. Maybe I'll turn out to be some great cook or something. I'll go along with it for her."

"That's okay, man," Kambui said. "And if it turns out really good you can cook something for me. But I don't eat ducks."

"Zander, are you free for lunch?" This from Caren Culpepper when I was sitting in the media center.

"Why?" This from me.

"I need to talk to you about something," Caren said. "I just need to get some things clear in my head."

"What things?"

"I'll meet you in the lunchroom in front of the popcorn machine," she said. "Twelve-thirty."

Caren started walking away and I was just telling myself that there was no way I was going to have lunch with her when Phat Tony from the Genius Gangstas came and plopped his overweight butt next to me.

"Hey, man, the people are talking that *The Cruiser* newspaper is lame compared to *The Palette*. You see the story they got this week?"

Phat Tony pushed *The Palette* in front of me. There was a picture of a woman soldier on the front page.

"They got an interview with her," Phat Tony said. "She killed two dudes over there and she just volunteered to go back again. Your little jive newspaper ain't got nothing like that, man. That's a collector's edition. All you got in your newspaper is whining and poems and stuff. You got a lame newspaper."

I knew, sooner or later, that I was going to have to go to war with Phat Tony. The dude just got on my nerves. I picked up the copy of *The Palette* he had pushed before me and turned to the article by the soldier. She wrote about how she wanted to defend her country and how her parents were nervous about her being in a combat zone and how she had been caught in an ambush and had to fire her weapon. What she said was she might have killed somebody, and maybe even two people. She said she wasn't happy with the idea but she had to do what she had to do. It was a strong piece, especially with the photograph.

I didn't have anything to say to Phat Tony because he wouldn't have understood it, anyway. The fool had a high IQ but I knew that didn't make him smart in any kind of useful way. He had stink breath, too.

THE CRUISER

A SPECIAL EDITORIAL

THE SAME STORY, A DIFFERENT VIEW

By Sagal Shehabi

The other day a young woman wrote a guest editorial in *The Palette*. I saw her in the school hallways. She was tall, for a woman, and blond, and quite beautiful. She spoke of serving in the military, and there was pride in the way she talked about doing her duty and using her weapon when she felt that was necessary. She was serving in a land with which I am familiar, because I was born there.

There is chaos in my land, my Afghanistan. People die almost every day and in every manner possible. Shiites kill Sunnis, Sunnis kill Kurds, Kurds kill Shiites. The Taliban kill at will. It goes on and on. No one in Kandahar is untouched. For us there are few heroes, and fewer heroines. A bomb is thrown onto a bus, unmindful of whose life it will take. A soldier shoots into a crowd, the bullets spreading destruction according to the rules of physics, not humanity.

When I was hit by a fragment of a bomb it was not me who was the target. The pilot of the plane did not know who I was or who my family was. He didn't know that I was only five and had just learned to read, or that I was the first girl in my family who had gone to school. Or that I cried all that night as my grandmother held me. Or that I was so frightened that I did not even look up into the air for the next week.

I have nothing against the young woman who came to Da Vinci and told how she had been a soldier. I just wanted to say that there are other sides to the same story.

CHAPTER TEN

Easy Does It

By lunchtime I was feeling low. Nothing was really breaking me down, but nothing was looking too cool, either. I was drifting off into Self-Pity City when Caren Culpepper and Zhade Hopkins came to where I was sitting. Zhade sat next to me (she was actually touching me!). I was surprised because I had forgotten that Caren had asked me to meet her.

"What's up?" Me, being lame.

"Caren said that you won't go out with her because you don't like her father and everybody's saying that if the Cruisers are so cool why are you putting down people's families?"

"What?"

"You didn't hear me?" Zhade asked.

"Yeah, I heard you." I looked over to where Caren was

staring dead at me with her head to one side like she was daring me to say the wrong thing. "We weren't even talking about going out."

"So, you going to go out with me or *what?*" Caren asked.

"You want to go out?" I asked.

"She's here, isn't she?" Zhade said, looking at me all serious. "Or are you too macho to have a girl ask you out?"

I felt like I was between the devil and the deep blue sea. On one hand I didn't want to go out with Caren again because the last time I went out with her she put it out that I was sweating her big-time, which was a lie. On the other hand, what was Zhade's play? I wasn't sure if I was setting up a date with Caren or her. At any rate, I said I'd go out with Caren, hoping that it was going to lead to a date with Zhade.

"Friday," Caren said. "The day after you guys put on the play."

She was already standing up, and I looked at Zhade and she was standing, and she had this really satisfied look on her face.

"Zander, you're a good dude," she said.

Then they were gone.

I saw Kambui in Biology and told him what happened.

"The same thing happened to a paramecium I was raising," Kambui said. "Two lady paramecia got him in the locker room and sexually molested him."

"Yo, Kambui, that is so seriously stupid I don't know how you can get it into your mouth to spit it out."

"I ain't going out with the assistant principal's daughter," Kambui said. "You are."

I got home and Mom was shopping on the Home and Garden Network. In between her buying everything I told her what happened.

"Zhade was bringing in stuff about me being macho and getting up in my face like it was her that I was going out with or something. I was really confused."

"Both of them like you," Mom said. "They're just going about letting you know in different ways."

"Neither one of them said anything about liking me," I said.

"They didn't have to," Mom answered. "You're easy. Hey, there's nothing wrong with that, because you're a guy. But, baby, you are easy. Right?"

"No!"

THE CRUISER

A LETTER

By Demetrius Brown

Please excuse me because my English is still not as good as it should be. But my friend Tyree Jackson was arrested this week and it looks as if nobody cares. He was caught shoplifting in a large store downtown. The police had pictures of him stealing wallets from the men's department and they caught him outside of the store. The thing that bothers me is that Tyree is a good person. Sometimes a good person does bad things. I know this.

What bothers me even more was that everyone at school knew what had happened on the same day that Tyree was arrested and nobody did anything about it. I don't know what Mrs. Maxwell did or what Mr. Culpepper did, but I know the students did not do anything.

I ask you this question. Did Tyree stop being Tyree? Do we stop loving people because they have made a mistake?

I did not expect a story to appear in the pages of *The Palette*. The editor of that paper is very smart but does not feel much. I did expect a story to be in *The Cruiser*.

I don't know what I will do, but I will reach out to Tyree, because he is someone I care about, as I care about all the world.

THE PALETTE

A Reply to Demetrius Brown
By Ashley Schmidt

I have read the letter that Demetrius Brown published in *The Cruiser*, and while I sympathize with Tyree, he was *caught* stealing and stealing is *wrong*! I am sorry that he stole, but I can't bring my heart to feel for him. It is not that I am unfeeling, Demetrius, it is because I know the difference between right and wrong!

THE CRUISER, SPECIAL EDITION

A REPLY TO ASHLEY SCHMIDT

By Zander Scott

Hey, Ashley, lighten up! If you look at people only by what they have done in the last few hours or few days then you are looking at a very small part of each person. That might fit *The Palette*'s idea of what a human being amounts to, but it doesn't fit mine. As Demetrius says, sometimes even good people can do bad things at times. When someone does do something bad or against the law we want to walk away like we are perfect. The Cruisers will look into the matter and I'm sure Mrs. Maxwell, Mr. Culpepper, and Tyree's teachers will as well.

I'm glad that you know the difference between right and wrong. I guess having faith in your fellow human beings is not part of your "right" thinking.

CHAPTER ELEVEN

Eye of Newt, and Toe of Frog

So this recipe is like a road map to get to a supper for twelve people," Kambui said. "So me and LaShonda are in the backseat reading the directions and everybody else is following our directions, right?"

"Right!" Mom said.

Me, Mom, and Bobbi were going to do the actual cooking, which I liked, because if it came out good I wanted to get credit for it.

"Cut the *ventrèche* into one-half-inch squares," Kambui said.

The *ventrèche* looked like rolled-up bacon, and I started cutting it up. We had soaked the white beans overnight like the recipe said and boiled them until they were almost done, and they were in a big pot on the stove. I got the *ventrèche* all cut up and Mom put it in a bowl.

"Season beans with salt and pepper!" Kambui said.

Bobbi put some salt and pepper on the beans. She looked serious. I liked that.

"Place half of the beans in the pot. Add the duck legs, the duck sausages, *ventrèche*, and garlic sausage, then pile on the rest of the beans," LaShonda said. "This sounds good!"

The kit we had bought had all the parts labeled, and Bobbi and Mom found all the duck legs and sausages they were talking about and put them into the pot.

"Mrs. Scott, I don't have any idea how this is going to come out," Bobbi said.

Mom shrugged. She didn't know, either.

"Mix tomato paste into dissolved demi-glace," Kambui said. "Then pour it over the beans."

We did that.

"Drizzle duck fat over everything."

"This recipe is not politically correct," LaShonda said. "You don't drizzle fat over food and think you're being cool."

I drizzled the duck fat. I didn't think I was being cool. I wasn't sure what I was being.

But after a while I could see everybody settling into their

attitudes. LaShonda started helping out with the cooking, and Mom sat down. I didn't want to sit down because I didn't think just the girls should be doing the cooking.

The pot we had wasn't big enough, and I had to go downstairs and borrow a pot from Mrs. Santana on the second floor. When she heard what we were doing she came up and started sniffing around.

"It smells like it's going to be all right!" she said.

By the time we put the pot in the oven, it was already smelling like something delicious and I was getting a little excited. Kambui was still trying to be cool, looking over the directions, but my layback had got up and walked out.

What I was seeing was that LaShonda was slowly taking over the kitchen. Bobbi was on top of things and they had me doing the cleaning up. Mom was getting to be a happy spectator and Mrs. Santana was talking about how her family used to cook together in San Juan.

"Everybody cooked!" Mrs. Santana said. "Abuela ruled the kitchen. She always had a wooden spoon in her hand and if you didn't do something right — *whack!* — you got hit. Then afterward we would all sit down and eat together and everybody would be laughing and talking because we had all helped."

Mrs. Santana was talking about being a family and I could feel what she was saying. In a way, that was what LaShonda was saying, too, and I wished I had thought about asking her to bring her brother over.

Mom wasn't really into cooking that much, but I could tell she was glad to have us all over to the house. I wondered if that's what she missed not being with my father.

"We're going to have enough food to feed an army," she said. "Start thinking about who else we can have over."

It took almost three hours before the whole meal was finished. Me and Bobbi put our table together with a card table and covered them both with a big tablecloth while Mrs. Santana put on some yellow rice. We got the table set and put out all our plates while Kambui started calling around inviting people to dinner.

Who we had over:

I asked LaShonda to call Chris and she did, but she had to get Mom on the phone to ask someone to bring him to our place. Mrs. Askew, from St. Francis, came with him.

Kambui's grandmother came over and said that the apartment smelled like "the back door to heaven." Mrs. Owens was really short but kind of wide and friendly.

The last person to show up was Mr. Santana.

"Don't speak nothing but English!" Mrs. Santana told her husband.

"Voy a hablar inglés! No se preocupe!" he answered.

There were ten of us altogether when we sat down to eat. Mrs. Owens said grace, and we dug in.

It was good. I didn't like the duck that much and the sausages didn't taste like I thought they would, but it was all okay. Mrs. Santana liked it the most, or maybe Mr. Santana did, but he just sat there eating and mumbling in Spanish.

Mrs. Askew thought the meal was "creative" and "a memorable experience." Whatever. In the end we had pulled off making a dinner, had eaten some stuff that was good but that we would probably never eat again, and had a new topic to talk about.

Chris sat next to LaShonda and I could see them together, almost as if it was some kind of dance. LaShonda smiled at us and talked when she was supposed to, but all the time she was moving along with her brother. When his arms got to swinging too wildly she held them down. When he began to open and close his hands very quickly, she took both of his wrists and brought his palms close so that they touched. Once she passed her hand in front of his face in a downward motion. It was a dance so subtle that it was almost invisible.

Chris never looked directly at anyone. He was an alien among us and we were aliens to him. I knew then that LaShonda was stronger than I could ever be — than I would ever want to be.

For a moment I was loving on LaShonda, thinking that maybe I would grow up and marry her. Then I thought about Chris and how hard it would be and made myself think of something else. That was something I could do that I knew LaShonda couldn't. I could think of something else besides Chris.

I wondered how my father would have fit in, if he would have been comfortable.

Bobbi, Mom, Kambui, and me cleaned up. Mr. Santana fell asleep in a chair, and Mrs. Askew went with LaShonda and Chris back to St. Francis.

I felt really good. We had done something and it had meant something. Different things to different people, but it had all had some meaning to it.

Plus, I had a piece of an idea. I needed to think it through more and maybe talk it over with Kambui and LaShonda. I didn't want to talk it over with Bobbi because

I knew that if I did she would think it through in a heart-beat and piss me off.

I called Kambui and told him that the dinner, how we were all together like an extended family, was what LaShonda needed all the time and that maybe we could convince Mrs. Askew to do something about keeping LaShonda and Chris together.

"You going to call her?" he asked, meaning he didn't want to call her.

"I'll think about it," I said.

Then I called LaShonda and told her my idea.

"She won't go for it," LaShonda said. "She's got guide-lines or something."

Then I called Bobbi.

"You think we should go to the Virginia Woolf Society and ask them to expand their program to include fami-lies?" she asked.

If you could really hate a squinty-eyed white girl who could think faster than a computer, Bobbi McCall was the one to hate.

THE PALETTE

A Reply to Zander Scott
By Ashley Schmidt

I am sorry that I wrote so hastily about Tyree Jackson. But there has to be a balance between individual responsibility and personal regard. We cannot offer excuses for bad behavior just because we like the person doing the offensive act or just because the person is usually not one to do bad things. I believe this and I stand by it. I am giving Alexander Scott an opportunity to reply in *The Palette*.

A Reply to Ashley Schmidt
By Zander Scott

We have to either judge people by their potential or we judge them by their circumstances. Ashley is saying it doesn't matter why someone does something if that something is wrong in her eyes. But she is setting herself up as a judge and jury. If someone in her family was starving and stole food to keep from dying, would Ashley then condemn that person?

No, she would excuse that behavior as "justified" because she understands the whole picture. Does she understand the whole picture with Tyree? Is she interested?

CHAPTER TWELVE
Wednesday's Child Is Full of Woe

So the plan was really simple. We would call the Virginia Woolf Society, tell them we wanted to have a conference, meet with them at their office, and Bobbi would tell them that they need to expand their offer to LaShonda to include all of St. Francis.

"And don't forget to smile a lot," Mom said. "Rich people feel comfortable when you smile."

The Cruisers were not about to go around smiling at people, but I didn't want to get up in Mom's face about it.

Kambui decided we should meet with them on Saturday afternoon, and me, LaShonda, and Bobbi agreed.

"They said they couldn't possibly meet with us on Saturday and that it would have to be either Wednesday or next month." Kambui was breathless and I knew the phone call hadn't gone well. "At four-thirty."

One good thing about Wednesday was that it was the day before we were going to put on our play for the community. If the play went badly we might be too down to talk to anybody.

Okay, so the Cruisers got together on Wednesday and hopped into a cab. Kambui gave the driver the address, but the man turned around, looked us over, and then asked if we were sure we had the money for the cab fare.

"Twelve dollars to Thirty-second Street!"

We got the money up and handed it over. I was thinking of saying something about did he know his way downtown but I thought he might put us out so I didn't.

We got to 31 East 32nd Street and told the guy in the lobby we had an appointment on the seventh floor. He gave us the same fishy look the cabdriver did.

"I think it's Kambui," LaShonda said. "He always did look a little sinister."

"That's true," Kambui said, punching the floor button with a sinister finger.

We got to the Virginia Woolf Society office and went into a room that looked like all you should do is whisper because if you spoke out loud something in the room would break. A thin woman pointed first toward a small couch and then to two leather chairs before disappearing behind a door with a frosted glass window.

"I guess she didn't think we could figure out we couldn't all sit on one chair," LaShonda said.

The room was full of books the same color as the leather furniture. I looked around and didn't see a paperback in the joint. After a while the frosted glass door opened and we were called into the room with a wave of the hand.

There were three women in the room sitting at a long desk, one on either end and the other one in the middle facing us. There were four chairs facing the table and I knew they had just been put there.

"I am Mary Brownstein, this is Elizabeth Poe, and this is Mrs. Turner, our board president. What can we do for you today?"

I turned toward Bobbi. She didn't move. I glanced over at LaShonda. She didn't move.

"We were thinking about LaShonda's going to live in the new place you have in Harlem," I said.

"This is the young lady I spoke to you about, LaShonda Powell, who has a flair for design." Mrs. Brownstein turned as she spoke to the woman who was the board president. "We believe she has *so* much potential."

"But . . ." For a moment I couldn't think of anything else to say. I wondered what Mr. Lord would have said.

"Yes?"

"The thing we were thinking is that everyone at Da Vinci has potential," I said. "And we were wondering —"

"We?" Mrs. Brownstein looked at LaShonda.

"We're known as the Cruisers," LaShonda said. "We look out for each other. I have their backs and they have mine."

"I see." Mrs. Brownstein.

"What we see is that you've recognized how talented LaShonda is, and not many people do," I said. "But we were thinking that instead of just hooking up LaShonda, it might be better if you could give a hand to St. Francis, the group home she's living in now. That way you could help some of the other kids there show their potential, too. And in a way, that would help the entire community, too."

"That's very unselfish, but I wonder about the focus." Mrs. Brownstein sat back in her chair and looked over her glasses. "Wouldn't it be more advantageous to the other young people at this group home —"

"St. Francis," LaShonda said.

"Yes, wouldn't it be more advantageous just to show that such talent exists and to showcase it?" Mrs. Brownstein said.

"I don't think so," LaShonda said.

"If you don't think that all the kids in the home have potential —"

"St. Francis?" Mrs. Brownstein said.

"Yeah, then it's cool to snatch out one person and hold her up," I said. "But if you believe that they all have talent and they all have smarts, then it's just a matter of giving them all the opportunity. It's like our school. Everybody in the school is smart. Da Vinci just gives us a chance to show it."

"We're giving our play tomorrow night for anybody who wants to come to it," Kambui added. "So it's, like, a community thing."

"What will your play be about?"

"It's called *Act Six*, and it's what happens to several of Shakespeare's characters at some future date," Bobbi said.

"Why is it called *Act Six*?" At the other end of the table, Mrs. Turner, the board president, spoke for the first time.

"Because all of Shakespeare's plays had five acts," Mrs. Brownstein said quickly.

"And how would we be able to help St. Francis?" Mrs. Turner asked.

"They can't afford a full-time person to help raise funds to keep the place going," LaShonda said. "They have to keep going to the city for additional funds, and they think the city might cut them back so they can't keep paying the rent."

"And you're all right with not moving, LaShonda?" Mrs. Brownstein asked.

"I am, I really am. There are so many kids who have something on the ball there," LaShonda said. "I think a lot of them will do well if they have the chance."

"I'm still worried about the focus," Mrs. Poe said.

"Isn't Gerald Yorke looking for a position?" the board president asked. "He would be perfect working for this home and he's used to dealing with the city. This might work out quite nicely. We're having brunch with his uncle next week. I'll talk to him about Gerald."

Mrs. Turner stood up and the other two popped up right behind her and we knew the meeting was over. We were escorted to the hallway and Mrs. Brownstein gave LaShonda a hug.

"One day you'll have to design a gown for me!" she said.

"I sure will!" LaShonda beamed.

In the elevator:

"Bobbi, you were supposed to do the talking!" I said.

"I froze up!" Bobbi said. She was ready to cry. "I always freeze up unless I'm mad."

"I think we did all right," LaShonda said.

"At least they didn't say no."

"They're grown-ups," Kambui said. "They're going to do what they want to do, anyway."

"Where did you get all that talk about how everybody had talent and stuff like that?" LaShonda said.

"From that Lord dude when he was mouthing off," I said as we hit the street.

"That's not how he was meaning it, though," LaShonda said. "He was thinking you should dumb everybody down so we'd be equally behind."

We got to the subway and Bobbi found out she didn't have her bus pass. We went to one of the cops in the station and he said he couldn't let her in, but then a transit worker came over and let her go through the gate.

I thought we had done okay, too. We had presented our case and had the Virginia Woolf Society at least thinking about it.

"Yo, folks, I got something else to say," I said.

"Go on and say it," Kambui said.

"I'm proud to be a Cruiser."

FRIENDS

By Bobbi McCall

They don't have to ride white horses

Or come to my rescue when I'm down

They just need to be there when I turn

So I can see them standing behind me

When I'm needing

A someone or maybe two

They don't have to be brilliant

Or strong or fast

They can just slide along

Glide along

Like they did when they first

Cruised into my life

When they smiled at me

When we started our journey

On the high seas of friendship

CHAPTER THIRTEEN
The Play's the Thing

One thing about Mr. Lord, he doesn't give up easily. When our principal, Mrs. Maxwell, announced that we were going to give *Act Six* for the community, I thought it was over. But Lord showed up with his people and they came early to get front-row seats.

"Almost all of the seats are filled!" LaShonda was looking out from between the curtains. "I see some of the ladies from the Virginia Woolf Society there, too."

I didn't see them at first but then Kambui pointed them out in the middle seats on the left-hand side.

"You think Lord's people are going to stop the play?" Bobbi asked.

"Five minutes!" Miss LoBretto, our drama coach, called. The play was going to start on time if she could help it.

Then Mrs. Maxwell walked out onto the middle of the stage.

"Ladies and gentlemen, the teachers, administrators, and student body all join in thanking you for coming out to see our play tonight. We think you will be pleased and hope you will encourage our young people in their performances. They're a bit nervous tonight because they want to do well, and I *know* you want them to do well."

"Amen to that, sister!" An old black man was nodding his head.

I saw Mr. Lord look over to where the old man sat and throw down a halfhearted mean mug.

"Our children learn in school," Mrs. Maxwell went on, "but they also learn from the community. How you receive them will go far in teaching them how much they are appreciated."

"Preach it, sister!" The old man was getting into his thing.

"After the play is over, the students will answer any questions you might have," Mrs. Maxwell said. "And you'll see how much work they have put into this production."

"Suffer the little children!" The old man was nodding again.

"Can we give our children a big hand even *before* they perform to tell them how much we love them?"

"She's working it!" Bobbi said as the audience started applauding. I looked over at Lord and he had to go along with the program. He was applauding, too. Then he was whispering something to his people and I knew we were over.

With everybody behind us the play went better than it had before. People were laughing at all the right places and some were even talking to themselves about what was happening on the stage. At the end we got another big round of applause, and even Mr. Lord's people applauded for us.

During the question-and-answer period, one of the ladies from the Virginia Woolf Society rose and told everyone that LaShonda had designed and made the costumes, and she got a big hand over that.

What I was waiting for was Mr. Lord to step up and try to rain on everybody but it didn't happen. Like Bobbi said, Mrs. Maxwell had stopped him before he even got started.

I didn't expect Mrs. Maxwell to be so sneaky. Okay, she wasn't really sneaky but she knew how to deal when it was time to deal.

"I think we should do a puppet play next," Kambui said. "Then we could go to hospitals and perform for sick kids."

"I can make puppets!" LaShonda said.

I had a feeling we were going to be doing a puppet show.

The Cruisers shook hands with everybody in the audience and they gave us a lot of hugs and too many kisses.

"Aren't you that weatherman's boy?" a little dark-skinned woman with a squeaky voice asked me.

"Yes, ma'am."

"Well, I liked your play a lot and you could be in the movies," she said.

"Thank you."

"Was it about anything in particular?"

"It was just supposed to be funny," I said.

"Well, it wasn't funny, but you young people were trying your little hearts out and that's what counts," she said. "Don't stay out too late."

"Yes, ma'am."

I found Mom in the audience and we walked home together. She was happy with the play, too.

"I heard some people saying LaShonda should team up

with Beyoncé or somebody and open up a clothing store in Harlem," Mom said. "That's probably too hard a gig, really."

The phone was ringing when we got home. It was my father calling from Oregon. It was eight o'clock in New York and five out there. He told Mom he wanted to speak to me and she gave me the phone.

"Have you thought any more about an amount for your allowance?" he asked, very clearly and concisely.

"I was going to say sixteen dollars a week," I said. "But if I'm going to be making cass-oo-lays and stuff I'd better make that twenty dollars and fifty cents a week."

"Making *what*?"

"Cass-oo-lays," I said. "It's a French dish with duck and white beans from the hilly areas of France, south of Paris."

"Oh." This from my father.

Mom was grinning all over herself and I held up my hand so she could give me five.

"I have to go now," I said. "My theater group just put on a play for the community and I'm quite tired."

"Oh."

He said he would think about the amount. I imagined him writing it down and comparing it to the figure he had in mind.

Everybody called everybody at least twice to congratulate us and then we texted each other. By the time I got to Facebook somebody had already uploaded the program and said that the play was dynamite. They added that it was better than anything that Frederick Douglass Academy could do, which was true, but I was mad that they even mentioned FDA.

One time I figured out how much I spent a week and it was about $23, which I bummed off Mom. If I did get the $20.50 a week from my father, which would be $1,066 a year, which was the year they fought the battle of Hastings, I would almost be phat. Not quite, but I was getting there.

CHAPTER FOURTEEN
Are Wars Necessary?

Mr. Siegfried thinks he's slick. He's always trying to teach us something in a sneaky way. So that's why he got together with a teacher from some charter school in Jersey City to hold a debate. The debating team from Da Vinci was Bobbi McCall, Kelly Bena, Ashley Schmidt, Phat Tony Williams, and me, the Zander man. It was a stupid debate from the get-go because the topic was Are Wars Necessary? Everybody knows what the answer to that is supposed to be so we were figuring we would get a free ride out to Jersey City and just chill our way through the set. To make it even more stupid, the school from Jersey City had to argue that wars were not necessary and we were supposed to stand up and say they were.

"Then everybody is going to boo us and say that they're the winners," Bobbi said.

Which is the way I figured it was supposed to go, but I had never been to New Jersey, so it was all good.

We got to the school, which is on this big boulevard, and met their debating team. I think I could have beat up their whole team by myself. They had these two fly Indian girls, a black dude, and two scared-looking kids I couldn't tell what they were. We flipped a coin and we lost so we had to start the debate. Ashley was up first.

"My people are from a little country in Eastern Europe," she said. "We have been run over many times. During these times our people have been killed, put into camps, and displaced from their homes."

She went on to talk about how people weren't free to speak the truth if there were people over them who didn't want to hear that truth. She even talked about her own family and how some of them had been killed and some had just disappeared.

"We don't know what happened to them," Ashley said. "They were taken away in the middle of the night and we never heard from them again. This is why my people think that if we are ever invaded again we must go to war or forever be slaves."

That was strong and I was ready to go to war already.

The other team's debater came back with some fuzzy idea about how the possibility of war against Ashley's people made people think about it in the first place.

"If everyone in the world condemned war, if there was no glory to conquering another people, then we would not support leaders who would seek war as a solution to international problems."

The dude went on about how war was a global mentality kind of thing and we had to change that mentality. To me it was the same old same old. Bobbi was up for us next, but Phat Tony wanted to go and Bobbi let him. I thought it was a mistake because Phat Tony is dumb — in a smart kind of way — but dumb.

"My name is Tony and I ain't no phony and they call me Phat because I'll give you a fat lip, a fat jaw, and a fat head when I be beating your brains out and spreading them across the street so the pigeons can eat, and when I turn your head inside out and you hear all the people shout that the inside of your head all bloody and red looks like a Domino pizza with extra ketchup and all those little black things ain't olives but little pieces of my black past which have caught up to you and now you ain't nothing but a memory of what used to be and as you lay down dying with your nose on the cold cement with your head busted open and your body bent in ways you didn't even know it could fold and you realize for the first time that the world belongs to the strong and proud and not to the can't-we-all-just-get-along crowd and as your miserable life comes to a cease the only thing that'll come into your mind is later for peace! 'Nuff said!"

Mr. Siegfried was mad. He turned red and gave Phat Tony a look that would have killed a lot of kids. But that wasn't the worst thing that happened. The worst thing that happened was that Bobbi got the giggles and couldn't stop, and even Kelly put her head down and smiled. I decided to be good and stay above the whole thing but then I saw Phat Tony mean-mugging the kids from Jersey City and that was funny, but then Bobbi tried mean-mugging them, too.

Bobbi is barely five feet tall and her eyes are too squinty to mean-mug anybody. If she tries to mean-mug you she looks as if she's got her eyes completely closed.

The rest of the debate was stupid, just the way I thought it was going to be, and when it was time for us to go and we were supposed to shake hands with our hosts they didn't look us in the face.

The three judges all picked the Jersey charter school as the winner.

"I have *never* been so embarrassed by a group of students in my *entire* life!" Mr. Siegfried was saying as we passed through the Holland Tunnel. "You did not represent Da Vinci well, you did not represent New York City well, and you did not represent *yourselves* well."

Nothing we could say, really. We were busted, guilty, doing the perp ride back to Harlem, and we were just waiting for our sentences. I came up with an idea I thought would save the day.

"Mr. Siegfried, we were just trying to show how wars developed when people refuse to debate stuff," I said.

"Zander, shut up!"

I dug where he was coming from. For a while. Until exactly six-fifteen when I was checking out "What did the fish represent in Ernest Hemingway's *The Old Man and the Sea*?" and Mom banged on the door, opened it before I could say anything (again!), and announced that Mr. Lord was on a cable channel.

I went in to check it out and saw Lord wearing a shiny suit and a little African hat standing next to one of the ladies from the Virginia Woolf Society.

"Turn up the sound!" I said, looking around for the remote. Mom had it and turned up the volume.

"So I went to Mrs. Brownstein from the Virginia Woolf Society and asked her for her support not just for a few gifted children, but for our entire community!" Lord was saying. "And she has graciously agreed to expand their level of support to include as wide a range of programs as possible."

"Yes." Mrs. Brownstein looked a little nervous. "I did speak to Mr. Gourd this morning —"

"That's Lord."

"Yes, of course." Mrs. Brownstein moved her head away from Mr. Lord as she spoke. "And he agrees with the changes we have proposed to St. Francis."

"This is a result not just of my efforts, but the efforts of a *community* that has stepped forward!" Lord went on.

"That dirty —"

"Watch your language!" Mom put her hands over her ears.

Besides me, only Kambui had seen the interview, but by the next day we were all talking about it in school.

Bobbi said we should send an op-ed piece to the *Amsterdam News* exposing the truth.

Kambui said that we should picket Mr. Lord's office on 138th Street.

"I don't care what he says," LaShonda said. "St. Francis is really happy with me and Chris because they're going to get some additional funding from the Virginia Woolf people and they got this guy who's going to work part-time for them — for free — to help them raise more funds. If nothing else happens, me and Chris will be able to stay together until I get a job and get my own place."

"Amen to that," I said.

The question we were debating in Jersey City was if war was ever necessary. Lord seemed to think so. And he could make himself a winner even if he lost. Which he did. The Cruisers beat him fair and square but he turned it around to make it look like he was a winner.

It's hard to tell who wins sometimes. Phat Tony thought he won in Jersey City even though our team lost. I thought the Cruisers had beat down Mr. Lord but he was declaring himself the winner.

LaShonda won in a way and in another way she didn't win because her situation was still bad. It just didn't get any worse and I guess that can be a win sometimes.

Mom won when we made the duck thing but when we were sitting around the table it wasn't our true family, just a made-up family of the Santanas, the Cruisers, Chris, Mrs. Owens, and Mrs. Askew. But it was something she could say to my father that we did together and that was something. Maybe that's what life was all about, finding something to say was a win.

CHAPTER FIFTEEN
My Date with Caren Culpepper

We go to a movie. Right in the middle of the movie she reaches over and takes my hand. I pull away. Then she leans against me. I move away. I remembered that the last time we went out she came back to school and said I was all over her, so this time I wasn't even going to get close.

Then she got near me and tried to kiss me on the cheek. I got away faster this time.

"Zhade said you were scared of girls," Caren whispered into the side of my face.

Then she kept making like she was laughing but covering it up with her hand so I wouldn't notice. Only I had to notice because she kept doing it.

I said I had to go to the bathroom. I went and texted Kambui and told him what was going down.

What should I do?

Man up!

What was that supposed to mean?
I texted LaShonda.

Kiss her!

Typical girl response.
I texted Bobbi.

Kiss her, Zander. I got your back!

I went back to my seat. I put my arm around Caren and when she looked up at me I went to kiss her. She turned away at the last moment and I kissed the back of her head.

I had the definite feeling that I had just lost big-time. But it was a nice kind of feeling.

ACT SIX

By Zander Scott

Romeo	Zander Scott
Juliet	Bobbi McCall
Iago	Cody Weinstein
Othello	Kambui Owens
Hamlet	Demetrius Brown

Scene: a small office in Midtown Manhattan. DR. IAGO
WILLIAMS sits behind an ornate wooden desk. On either side
of the desk sit ROMEO and JULIET.

IAGO

So, what brings you to marriage counseling?
Perhaps you can begin, Miss . . . ?

JULIET

Montague, Juliet Montague. To put it mildly, we've
grown apart. I mean, really, really, REALLY apart.
Romeo hasn't had a job in years, and —

ROMEO

Neither have you, baby! We get by because my
family has a little money. Don't leave that part out.

JULIET

Money wouldn't make my life any better, Romeo. I am bored out of my mind! Out of my mind! All that he does is to come home at all hours in the morning, sleep until noon, and then get up in time for lunch and his stupid video games.

IAGO

But besides being bored, Juliet, I need to know your inner feelings toward your husband.

JULIET

I see this man and his potbelly in the morning, I see him in the afternoon. I watch television in the evenings BECAUSE I'M HOME BY MYSELF! And then the whole thing starts over again the next day. I can't remember the last time we went out to dinner. He acts as if he doesn't even know that I exist.

ROMEO

I'm a free spirit. You used to like that in me. You thought it was romantic when I stayed out all night. I remember the first night I climbed up on your balcony. Do you know what time it was? Two o'clock in the morning. You nearly swooned.

JULIET

You couldn't even climb up a fire escape these days. You're so out of shape you're sagging in places some people don't even have places! And he dresses like a slob. Tights? At his age?

IAGO

I'm hearing anger, but I'm not hearing communication. Have you tried sitting down and talking to each other?

ROMEO

She won't listen.

JULIET

Try me!

ROMEO

Okay, so what I'm trying to say is that I haven't changed over the years. I'm still the same happy-go-lucky guy I always was. Happy-go-lucky but ready to give my life for the girl I love.

JULIET

The girl you loved has grown into the woman who

is tired of you, Romeo. Look, read my lips. I am very much exhausted with the idea of being married to a juvenile delinquent.

IAGO

Well, you know, some marriages just don't work out. I mean, I would hate to see the two of you break up. To me marriage is sacred . . . precious . . . divine . . . blah, blah, blah. But there must be happiness within the home. And there must be a meeting not only of the hearts, but the minds as well. Look, I'm going to leave the room and I want you both to pour out your hearts to each other. Say everything you've been holding back.

IAGO stands and exits right. JULIET glances over at ROMEO, then rolls her eyes upward.

ROMEO

Look, Juliet. I don't want to be just another statistic. Last year, 14,000 people got divorced, leaving 23,000 children in broken homes!

JULIET

We don't have children.

ROMEO

We could buy a dog.

JULIET

So I can walk him and pick up his poop? That's
what I'm being reduced to? A pooper-scooper?

ROMEO

Shouldn't we be talking about *our* problems, not
just *yours*? You being bored is not a problem for
me. I didn't even mention the fact that you're fat
because —

JULIET

I'm fat? I'm fat? I thought you didn't even care
about how I looked. What happened to all of that
stuff about me shining like a diamond in the ear of
some black dude? How about me being lovelier
than the moon? Now I'm fat? You don't take me out,
all I do is sit around the house all day, and the one
thing I have going on (begins to cry), the one thing I
have going on is a few tidbits in the afternoon.

ROMEO

Bowling! You want to go bowling?

JULIET

The romance of it overwhelms me. A bowling alley
reeking with the stink of beer. I wear a pair of
sweaty rented shoes over the sticky floor, throw a
ball down the alley, and all of a sudden my whole
life is reset?

ROMEO

No, we do it in the comfort of our own living room.
I can get the video game tomorrow. We hook
ourselves up and we control the whole game. You
see what I mean?

JULIET

Let's call Dr. Iago back in here. Some marriages
need to be broken up, and I think this is one
of them.

ROMEO

So you're saying, once and for all, that you don't
love me?

JULIET

Love I'm not sure about. What I am sure about is
that I can't stand you!

ROMEO

Tell me, is there someone else?

JULIET

Like who?

ROMEO

I don't know, but I can't see how you can just walk
away from what we had. I mean, mostly *(profiles)*, me!

JULIET

My family was right. I should have listened to them.
You Montagues don't have a clue.

Enter IAGO.

IAGO

So, how are we doing?

ROMEO

Uh, not so good. But we're working on it. She's
learning to communicate.

JULIET

I'm learning? You are such a —

IAGO (quickly)

We have to remember that not all marriages are made in heaven. Sometimes . . . well, sometimes we need to consider other options. Especially when it's clear that the woman couldn't possibly love the man involved.

ROMEO

Couldn't possibly?

JULIET

That's a little strong, isn't it, Iago?

IAGO

Romeo, you have loved wisely, but far too well. For love is a smoke made with the fume of sighs that lead us all to hell.

ROMEO

I see what you mean.

JULIET

You can't be saying there's no hope for us? I mean, aren't you supposed to be saving marriages?

IAGO

Well . . . yeah, okay. Look. As we've agreed, I've
invited some of your friends over, the ones you've
already been talking to about your marriage, to
ask their opinions. I'll send them in.

ROMEO

Oh, okay.

JULIET

I'm sure that . . . well, okay.

IAGO leaves.

Enter HAMLET.

JULIET

Oh, great. Hamlet, the king of gloom himself.

HAMLET *(gloomily)*

Hi, Julie. Hi, Rommy.

JULIET

Hamlet, it's Juliet and Romeo. Not Julie and
Rommy. Do we call you Ham?

ROMEO

Yo, sit down, my man. What's up?

HAMLET

I got a new job, I'm selling condos now.

JULIET

In this market? You working on commission?

HAMLET

Yeah, kind of. I get one percent of the final sale or
two percent, whichever is higher. It's pretty tricky.
Math, percentages, that kind of thing.

ROMEO

Remember I told you what the marriage counselor
said about asking our friends if our marriage can
be saved?

HAMLET

Well, if you still think she's a fat pig and kind of
stupid, then I —

JULIET

A fat pig? Kind of stupid!?

ROMEO

No, no, I didn't mean any of that. I just said it that
time you locked me out. It wasn't personal.

JULIET

Not personal? When you call your wife a fat pig it's
personal, Romeo friggin' Montague!

HAMLET

If you broke up you could buy two separate
condos. As it turns out, I only have two left. A
studio on the ground floor, apartment
1A, and a two-bedroom luxury suite on the
second floor with a built-in spa. Apartment
2B, just right for whoever gets the bigger
settlement.

ROMEO

So you're thinking we should actually break up?
After all these years?

HAMLET

Unless you want to share the luxury suite. It's got
two bedrooms, so if you still hate the way she
snores you could just —

JULIET

Hate the way I snore!? You told Hamlet about
what goes on in our bedroom?

ROMEO

Words, words, mere words. All I know is that
heaven is here, where Juliet lives.

JULIET

O Romeo, Romeo! Wherefore art thou, Romeo?
Sometimes I look at you with such delight, but
sometimes you're as fickle as a candle wavering in
the night.

Then there's a knock and enter OTHELLO.

OTHELLO

Hey! What it is! Am I late?

JULIET

Othello Jones. Oh, my God! It's been so long!

OTHELLO

When I heard you needed me I dropped
everything and came running. Feast your eyes,

darling. It's me, Othello Jones, the OJ man himself at your service.

ROMEO

Who is this Othello guy?

JULIET

Er, just an old friend?

ROMEO

From school?

OTHELLO

Yeah, I taught her a few things. Did her flaming youth let virtue be as wax and melt in her own fire? And were you consumed by her heat? Now you know how she learned her skills.

JULIET

Othello, did Dr. Iago tell you why we're here today?

OTHELLO

Yeah, you're looking for a reason to ditch this dude. Like you said in Las Vegas, we had something going on that he can't even touch.

HAMLET

Do you live in Vegas? You could move to New York
into a great little condo.

ROMEO

Las Vegas? I thought you went to Las Vegas to that
cosmetic convention with the girls — the Avon
ladies or something?

JULIET

They couldn't make it.

ROMEO

All five thousand of them?

JULIET

Don't overreact.

ROMEO

I'm not overreacting, I just don't confuse the word
"convention" with the word "rendezvous"!

JULIET

Romeo, when you think about it, a convention *is* a

kind of rendezvous. It's just a name. I mean, a
name, a *name*. What's in a name? A rose by any
other name would smell as sweet.

HAMLET

Something smells rotten here. I think the two of you
should break up.

OTHELLO

But as far as you two breaking up, I'm against it.
Things broken in two are not easily put together
again.

HAMLET

If you're going to stay together you need the
condo. It's 2B or not 2B. If you stay together, it's got
to be 2B.

JULIET

So what's your vote, Hamlet? We stay together or
we break up?

HAMLET

What's your credit score?

ROMEO

I'll — I'll take that as a no! We won't break up.
Juliet, I love you. *(falls to one knee)* And I've
always loved you!

JULIET

You're on your knees and you're begging me, but
you've done that before and nothing's changed.

ROMEO

This time it'll be different, my love. This time I'm
coming from a different place, from the very
bottom of my heart.

JULIET

Yeah, yeah, the light is breaking through the
window and I'm the sun. I've heard it all.

ROMEO

Look, I've gone more than halfway on this. I'm not
the one hanging with the homeboys!

OTHELLO

I hear the echo of the green-eyed monster. It's
time I excuse myself from this sorry crowd.

JULIET

Let's call Iago back and tell him what happened,
but also that we want to stay together. Romeo, I
do love you.

HAMLET and OTHELLO leave and IAGO reenters.

IAGO

And what have we decided?

ROMEO

We love each other and we're staying together, no
matter what.

JULIET

Love lifts itself like a banner above our heads
and we bravely follow! If life is indeed a battle
then we are armed with sweet affection one for
the other.

ROMEO

I'll get a job!

JULIET

And for me a tummy tuck.

IAGO

O what a curse is marriage! That two young people drown happily in the sea of love while older, wiser souls sit barren by the cliffs. But in the end they will grow old and fat while my solitude holds me forever firm and fast. It is my nature's plague to spy into abuses and oft my jealousy shapes faults that are not. Still, looking upon their glowing faces, they will not understand their defeat. Ah, what fools these mortals be!

The End

COMING UP NEXT . . . THE FOURTH BOOK IN THE CRUISERS SERIES

OH, SNAP!

In the next book of the Cruisers series, when Ashley Schmidt, the editor of The Palette, *decides to upgrade the school's official newspaper by running articles from the British paper* The Guardian, *the Cruisers respond by adding "across the pond" stories in their own paper. They begin a serial story, invite guest articles by kids from a gifted and talented school in London, and add photos to their paper. But when Kambui photographs a group of kids at the mall, it leads to major complications.*

Check out this excerpt:

OH, SNAP!

So let me get this straight," Bobbi said. "You were just taking random shots and you saw Phat Tony and snapped a picture without saying anything to him?"

"Because every time he sees a camera, he starts mugging and putting on his gangster poses," Kambui said. "I was just looking for casual shots."

"Right, and now you have a casual shot of Phat Tony with those three dudes they arrested for sticking up the jewelry store in the mall," LaShonda said. "The papers said that they got three of the holdup guys, but one got away. Isn't that what we read, Zander?"

"Yes, but we don't know that Phat Tony was the fourth guy," I said. "And they're pleading innocent, anyway. They said they weren't even at the mall that night."

"So what do we do?" Bobbi said. "We keep the photograph to ourselves and let them get away with a crime?"

"Or do we turn the photograph over to the police and get them *and* Phat Tony arrested?" I asked.

"We don't know that Phat Tony was the guy with them," Kambui insisted.

"What we know, Kambui, is that something bad happened at the mall and that we might have the key to it," I said. "Now we have to figure out what our responsibility is and to whom. Do you feel right just doing nothing?"

And that's the dilemma. The Cruisers have a photograph that could absolutely be the key to a conviction, but will it also be a conviction for Phat Tony, the loud, bragging, but usually good-doing student at Da Vinci? Should they be the hidden jury that convicts or frees someone who has committed a felony? And even if Phat Tony wasn't involved, do the Cruisers really feel safe in providing evidence against a desperate crew of robbers?

About the Author

Walter Dean Myers is the critically acclaimed *New York Times* bestselling author of nearly one hundred books for children and young adults. His extensive body of work includes *Sunrise Over Fallujah*, *Fallen Angels*, *Somewhere in the Darkness*, *Slam!*, *Jazz*, and *Harlem Summer*. Mr. Myers's many awards include two Newbery Honors, five Coretta Scott King Author Book Awards, the first Michael L. Printz Award, and the 2010 Coretta Scott King–Virginia Hamilton Award for Lifetime Achievement. In addition, he the 2012–2013 National Ambassador for Young People's Literature. He lives in Jersey City, New Jersey.